"Fixing cars is a .... for a girl. How'd you ever get into it?" Billy asked, looking straight into Alison's eyes. She shivered slightly, even though there was a warm breeze.

"My old boyfriend, Marty Willins, taught me everything I know."

"Marty Willins, the driver?" Billy seemed impressed. "I've heard of him. He was a really good racer, until—" Billy paused, not quite sure of how to finish his sentence. He awkwardly made a circle in the dust with the toe of his sneaker.

"Yeah, until his accident," Alison finished for him, aware that for the first time in the year since Marty died, she didn't feel upset when she spoke those words. The loneliness of that long year had suddenly dissolved into wonderful images of working with Billy Kendall. She'd been solo for too long.

Love In The Fast Lane

Rosemary Vernon

BANTAM BOOKS
TORONTO · NEW YORK · LONDON · SYDNEY

RL 6, IL age 11 and up

LOVE IN THE FAST LANE
A Bantam Book / July 1984

ISBN 0-553-24151-6

Published simultaneously in the United States and Canada

---

*Bantam Books are published by Bantam Books, Inc. Its trademark,
consisting of the words ''Bantam Books'' and the portrayal of a
rooster, is Registered in U.S. Patent and Trademark Office and in
other countries. Marca Registrada. Bantam Books, Inc., 666 Fifth
Avenue, New York, New York 10103.*

Printed and bound in Great Britain by Hunt Barnard Printing Ltd.

O   0 9 8 7 6 5 4 3 2 1

*Special thanks to Michael and
Jon-Pierre Levesque
for their valuable information on motocross.*

Love In
The Fast Lane

Chapter One

"Hey, what do you think you're doing?" Alison Matlock snapped, dragging Jeff Cutler away from the open hood of the car. "Trying to kill us both?"

Jeff was about to undo the radiator cap of his overheated car without waiting for the steam to die down. His car had suddenly started to sputter and finally chugged to a stop, steam pouring out of the engine. Jeff had swaggered over and lifted the hood as though he were Mr. Mighty Mechanic.

"You obviously don't know the first thing about cars," Alison continued. It was unlike her to be so snotty, but Jeff was really too much. If there was one thing she couldn't stand, it was a know-it-all boy—especially when it came to cars. Alison had been rebuilding engines before she could even drive them, and when Jeff pretended that he was going to save helpless Alison, her patience gave out.

1

She stood with her hands on her hips, her big brown eyes narrowed, and said, "Go ahead, try fixing this car yourself and see whether you make it home by Monday morning. As for me, I'm leaving. Good night." With that she turned away from Jeff, his gaping mouth, and his steaming car and walked briskly away.

It had not been a fun evening from the start. Sure, Jeff was popular and handsome. A lot of girls would have loved to have been in Alison's shoes that night. Jeff was one of these all-around talented boys, one who had a charming smile and always won student council elections and played the leads in school musicals. He had asked Alison out only after a lot of pressure and hinting from her friend, Heather, whose brother was Jeff's best friend.

Such set-ups never worked. They always made Alison feel at a disadvantage—like some poor, lonely soul who needed help in meeting boys and going out on dates. She had never seen herself like that before. Her natural good looks and quick smile had always rewarded her with lots of friends. But after Marty, she had found herself wanting to be alone more and more, not smiling quite so often and only going through the motions of being interested in meeting people and doing things.

"Oh, Marty, I miss you," Alison whispered into the dark night as she walked toward the bus stop. How many times in the past year had she murmured the same thing?

Marty had been her first love. "Soul mates" was what everyone had called them. Ever since he had moved next door to Alison when she was in first grade and he was in third, they had been friends. Alison was adventurous, and was willing to do anything Marty did. Their friendship had blossomed into a romance when Alison began ninth grade.

Marty and Alison were exactly alike. They both loved challenges and excitement and fun. It was Marty who had taught Alison all about cars—and every boy she met after Marty seemed boring and bland by comparison.

She thought about the hours she had spent huddled under the hoods of cars with Marty. The image of his face, black with grime and grease, grinning up at her as he slid out from under a car, brought a slight smile to Alison's face. He was so happy-go-lucky and free. Marty never seemed to be afraid of anything—whether it was tackling a new

3

problem with an engine or racing toward a challenging finish line.

Marty had been a stock-car racer—and a really good stock-car racer, too. He had won so many races that it was a wonder that his trophies meant anything at all to him. Part of Marty's success had been that he was as safe as he was fast. That was what made his last race such a shock. Marty didn't believe anything terrible could ever happen to him when he was racing—and, as a result, neither did Alison.

She wished she could know if he was afraid just before he died. There were three days of agony as he lingered in a coma, somewhere between life and death. She had put all of her energy into giving life to Marty during those three days, whispering, "Live, live, live" continuously. But Marty needed more than words to live.

Alison had lost her best friend and her only love. She kept thinking that if she hadn't been in love with Marty, she wouldn't feel so much pain now. Her friends, especially her two best friends, Heather and Julie, tried to keep her from withdrawing and building a protective shell around herself. They set her up with dates and always included her in their plans. Alison had seen almost every movie that had come to town and been to lots of concerts. Heather and Julie had practically become her sisters. They came over all the time, and they made sure she stayed in the swing of things.

But in spite of their efforts, Marty was continually on Alison's mind. It had been exactly one year since he had died. She hadn't had another steady boyfriend, and her blind dates seemed absurd when she recalled Marty. They had known each other so well, had really clicked. And sometimes they seemed to know what the other was thinking without uttering a single word.

The one thing that still didn't seem absurd to Alison was working on a car. She loved to dig into a sick engine, thinking logically and mechanically to solve its problem. The results of her work were immediate and always satisfying. Cars were a part of Marty that Alison had to hang on to—all but the racing of them, that is. She had never been back to a race track. The thought of cars zooming around a track was now a nightmarish memory.

Her daydreaming was interrupted by a sudden squeal of tires and a screech of brakes.

At first she was afraid that the car pulling up next to her was Jeff's. Maybe he had fixed it and was now coming to flaunt his success as a mechanic. But instead a cheerful-looking boy with red hair stuck his head out of the open window of a pickup truck. Alison had never seen the driver before, a guy about her age who had a welcoming grin on his face.

"It's pretty late to be walking alone. Need a lift somewhere?" he asked.

Instinctively Alison refused and kept walking, her eyes on the road in front of her.

The voice said, "Your choice. Maybe some other time. Be safe, now."

Alison stared longingly after the rear lights, disappearing around the bend. It wasn't that she minded walking. It wasn't that late, and there were several couples out walking and enjoying the warmth of the April night. But there was something about that open smile and the friendly, songlike voice. She was sure she could have trusted that boy for a ride home. Just for an instant she had forgotten the misery of her evening.

Well, at least I'm not a basket-case, she thought as she boarded the bus. *Some things can still cheer me up a bit.*

* * *

"It looks as if a man is going to help you in the fulfillment of your dream," intoned Heather, running her fingers over a Tarot judgment card.

"Oh, give me a break, Heather," replied Alison. "That's what you tried to tell me about Jeff and look what happened with him. I made a total fool of myself."

Julie giggled and reached for another slice of cheesecake. The three friends all had the last period free on Fridays, and every week they would gather at Alison's to watch their favorite soap opera. Traditionally Julie would make some exotic but delicious food for the occasion. She was a great cook and constantly tried out new recipes and tested them on her friends.

Julie and Heather were opposites in almost every way possible. Julie was the practical problem solver, while Heather was more emotional and dreamy. Even physically they were opposites. Julie was short and needed to lose about fifteen pounds. Her short, curly hair matched her round body. Heather had long, blond hair, and her tall, lean body resembled a picket fence. But Heather was anything but gawky or stiff. She was devoted

7

to modern dancing and really knew how to move what little flesh she had.

Heather always brought her Tarot cards over on Fridays to entertain her friends during the commercials. Neither Julie nor Alison believed that the cards could foretell the future. They were convinced that Heather just used the cards as an excuse to give advice. But they always pretended to take her seriously.

"Get a load of this, Alison," Heather continued, not to be put off by her friends. "This is the three of cups. You have had serious doubts about your future happiness, but never fear. Because of some effort on your part and some chance happenings, including a mysterious visitor and the help of a man, you should have a happy answer to your burning question." Heather sat back with a self-satisfied smile.

"And what question might that be?" asked Alison. "I know my problems all too well. Seems like my biggest problem is that too many people are trying to give me answers. Anyway, are you trying to tell me to sit back and twiddle my thumbs, waiting for Prince Charming to come and rescue me? So much for all your efforts at matchmaking."

They were in one of the sitting rooms in

the inn that Alison's family had bought three years before. Her parents loved the inn in the Berkshire Mountains in Massachusetts. It had been a run-down eighteenth-century farmhouse when they had bought it. Alison's mother had transformed it into a modern, comfortable living space that retained its earlier charm. Each room was individualized with the antiques that Mr. Matlock collected. It had a homey and warm atmosphere.

The friends' chatter was interrupted by the phone.

"Maybe that's your Mr. Mystery right now," chimed in Julie. Her smile was teasing.

Alison picked up the phone, trying to answer in her most casual voice but half expecting some man to claim her as his queen then and there.

It was a guest of the inn, canceling the inn's only reservations for that night.

"No problem," replied Alison. "I hope you can make it some other time."

Alison was relieved when she hung up the phone. She helped out at the inn a lot, especially during the busy months and on weekends. Usually she enjoyed the work. But she had been wanting to put a new radiator in her father's Toyota for a few weeks. The cancellation meant that she would have time before dinner to run over to the junkyard and get started on the project. She could finally spend some time with her true love, a sick car.

Chapter Two

"Hi."

Alison turned in the direction of the voice. A boy walked toward her from a pickup that had just arrived at the junkyard gate.

"Want some help?" he asked when she didn't respond.

Alison was poised under the hood of an old Chevy, disconnecting the radiator hoses. "I can do it, thanks," she replied, undoing the last bolt that held the radiator in place.

"Let me." He moved next to her, and she became aware of the mixed scents of motor oil and soap on him as he helped her hoist the radiator out of the car.

"Thanks."

"Where to?"

She pointed to the Toyota station wagon on the other side of the cyclone fence. They walked through an opening and over to the car. She spread newspapers inside the back of

11

the Toyota so that the boy could set the radiator down.

He was tall and the large muscles in his back and upper arms showed through his blue T-shirt. He wore a blue- and white-striped cap low over his brow, shading his freckled nose and hiding his hair. There was a little white scar shaped like a bow next to his mouth, which Alison focused on.

"Are you doing this job yourself?" he asked, looking straight at her with his dark brown eyes.

Alison shivered slightly even though there was a warm breeze. "Yes. That radiator is practically new."

"So I noticed. Are you good at fixing cars?" He seemed genuinely interested.

"I'm OK," she answered and shrugged, not wanting to appear immodest.

"How'd you ever get into it?" he asked.

"My old boyfriend, Marty Willins, taught me everything I know."

"Marty Willins, the driver?" The boy seemed impressed. "I've heard of him. He's a great racer. *Was*, I should say."

Alison nodded automatically but was silent and stared at the ground.

"Sorry." He made a circle in the dust with the toe of his sneaker.

"Yeah, me, too," she said softly.

"I'm looking for an engine," he said cheerfully, changing the subject. "Do you know where there are some late-model Fords?"

Alison took in his pleasant, wide grin, the sun that was slanting across his face, and the way he shoved his hands casually into his Levi pockets. With one foot leaning on a car bumper, he waited for her reply.

"They brought in a new Ford last week," she said, smiling. "Follow me."

"I need to get my pickup fixed, my dad's getting tired of me driving his. Then I'll be able to haul my bikes around again. Hey, this one looks great." He glanced inside the red truck, then yanked up its hood. "Only seventeen thousand miles on this thing. Not bad, huh? This is exactly what I've been looking for. My troubles are over."

"How do they get the engine out?" Alison asked.

"They cut it out with a blowtorch. Then I pick it up tomorrow." He grinned at her. "By the way, my name's Billy Kendall. What's yours?"

"Alison Matlock." He extended a freckled

arm to her, and she took his hand, warmed by his firm shake.

"Ever put in an engine before?" He was twisting sideways as he leaned into the truck's engine.

"No." Alison studied his back. "But I've always thought it would be interesting."

"Would you like to help me put this one in?"

"Well, sure." Alison wondered why she felt so comfortable talking to Billy. Maybe it was because the subject of cars and engines was so familiar.

"It's a grungy, two-day job—taking out and putting in. You probably know that already," he explained.

"I've got time, and I'm not afraid of grunge," she said.

He grinned. "I believe it. You're a rare bird." His eyes followed the line of her long brown hair, which spilled loosely over her shoulders.

Together, they walked up to the office, a ramshackle shed that cast a long shadow across the crumpled bodies of cars and trucks.

"That's one good deal you've got there," the owner of the junkyard told Billy with

14

enthusiasm. "I'm charging you three-fifty for it. I just got that truck in the day before yesterday."

"Sounds OK to me," Billy said. "Still cheaper than a new car."

The radiator Alison had just removed cost her twenty-five dollars.

"Both of us made out like bandits today," Billy remarked once they were outside. "Maybe we should work together. I can help you with the radiator after I get this engine in."

"OK. This weekend?" She hoped he didn't think she was too pushy, but she was suddenly enthusiastic about the idea.

"Yeah, sounds good. I'll give you a call early tomorrow morning. Are you in the book?"

"Yes."

"OK, Alison Matlock. See you then." He hoisted himself onto the truck seat, removed his cap in imitation of a true gentleman, and bowed his head in a goodbye flourish.

And what a flourish! Spilling out from under the cap was a mass of red curls. Unmistakable big, red corkscrew curls that flew everywhere without the containment of the cap. Billy Kendall was the boy who had stopped her on the road the night before!

What a coincidence, she thought, trying to close her mouth as he drove away, waving his arm out the window. Not only had she felt comfortable with him at the junkyard, she had even felt comfortable when he stopped for two seconds to ask her if she needed a ride home.

As she slid into her father's Toyota, Alison smiled to herself. *Maybe this is Heather's mysterious visitor,* she thought.

In the rearview mirror she watched Billy turn his truck out of the rutted road onto the state highway. She kept sight of it in the rearview mirror until the pickup disappeared in the flow of traffic that sped westward across the valley.

Yes, cars were a weird pastime for a girl, she reflected, gunning her motor. But then cars had been a big part of a very special friendship. She remembered that she and Marty had planned to put a new engine in his car after the race that turned out to be his last.

Funny how things happen, she thought, suddenly aware that her loneliness had dissolved as she imagined herself working beside Billy Kendall. She'd been solo for too long. . . .

Chapter Three

Alison fixed a bowl of ice cream for dessert and went to talk to her father in his office.

"I found a radiator at the junkyard, Dad. Your car will be like new in no time at all."

Tom Matlock had short-cropped, brown hair the same shade as Alison's. His features were sharp and distinguished. He glanced up from his bookkeeping to smile at his daughter.

"You're going to need a hand with it, aren't you? Buzz Tyler might be free this weekend—"

Buzz was a friend of the family who had helped Alison with a few repairs in the past year.

"No, Dad, I won't need help. I met a guy at the junkyard who's putting in an engine this weekend. I'm helping him with that, then he'll come over, and we'll do the radiator." Alison tried not to show her excitement.

"Sounds like a great way to spend the weekend," her father said, laughing. Working on cars was not his idea of relaxation.

"Things may be busy around here this weekend, Al," said her father, thinking about the inn. "If you can't work, will you see if Heather wants to take your place?"

Alison nodded and stared at her father poring over his long columns of addition. Suddenly she felt weary as she looked at her father's tired face. As much as he loved the inn, it was still hard work to run it. Even after dinner there was a lot of work to do.

Alison was the Matlocks' only child. Marty had been almost like a son to them, but now there was just Alison. They had tried to hide their own sorrow to help Alison recover. They hoped that by keeping her busy she would start to forget about the pain that she had been through.

"Al, come here a minute, will you? I want your opinion on this wallpaper!" Alison's mother poked her head around the corner and motioned to her.

"Sure." Alison followed her mother upstairs to the room she was redecorating. Wallpaper books were spread out on the floor near a swatch of rust carpeting. Her mother

18

was kneeling on her hands and knees, experimenting with different combinations. Like Alison, Marcy Matlock was slender and of average height and had delicate features. Her blond hair was naturally curly and fell in soft swirls about her face. She was active, fun, and casual, preferring sweat pants to a skirt any day.

"Which do you like better? The floral or the checks for this room?"

"The floral," Alison said. "It goes with the French print chair."

"You're right!" her mother exclaimed. "I never thought of that. I knew you'd save the day." She kissed Alison lightly on the cheek and absently asked about her day.

"I bought a radiator," Alison said, realizing how different she was from her mother, who barely knew how to use a self-service gas pump. Yet Alison had inherited a flair for decorating from her.

"Sounds thrilling, Al," Marcy Matlock said, laughing. "It'll be nice to get that car running right again, won't it? I'm sick of the knocks and pings."

"Yeah."

"Anyone helping?"

"A boy I met at the junkyard."

"Another grease monkey, huh?" her mother asked, giggling. "Sometimes I wonder about you."

"I think it'll be fun."

"Is he cute?"

"Is that all you ever think of, Mom?"

"Sorry. It's just that I worry about you."

"He's got two left feet, a crooked nose, and ears like Dumbo."

"You're such a tease. But you understand I want the best for you, don't you? You don't seem very interested in finding a boyfriend." She stacked the wallpaper books.

"There are not very good choices out there," Alison said, sighing. "I'd rather not waste my time."

Alison went downstairs to her bedroom, a large space with windows overlooking the back woods. The room was decorated in a blue bandanna print wallpaper, with matching bedspread and curtains. Alison had taken several photos of Marty's race car, and these hung in a cluster over her dresser. A collection of antique dolls sat at the end of her four-poster brass bed. She had started collecting them years before, when she went to antique auctions and flea markets with her father.

Alison changed into a pair of designer

jeans and a soft wool sweater. She was going to the movies with Heather and Julie. Alison tried on some eyeshadow and mascara—her complexion was smooth and clear, so she needed nothing else. She hadn't worn makeup in a long time, but somehow she felt like being a little prettier that night. "Just in case you bump into Billy Kendall again, huh?"

She laughed at her own silliness, but she was surprised at the warm glow she felt at the thought of running into Billy.

Julie and Heather breezed in. "It's so windy out there! I love it!" Heather exclaimed. "We ought to go kite flying tomorrow." Heather was the athletic one of the two.

"Hey, guess what? I'm going out with Barry Saturday night." Heather gave her friends a self-satisfied smile as they walked outside to Julie's car. Barry was the tallest boy in the eleventh grade. Heather was always looking for someone taller than herself.

"Are you still his lab partner?" Alison asked as they got into the car.

"Yes. We've been rubbing shoulders in chemistry for the last six weeks, which has helped us get to know each other. We talk about everything under the sun—except chemistry, of course. I've been sort of keeping him a secret."

"So we noticed."

"But he asked me if I wanted to see the new movie at the Windsor, and of course I said yes. I'm dying to see it."

"The Windsor doesn't play new movies," Alison noted.

Heather sighed. "It's an old movie we both missed."

"How romantic." Julie stared at the red light before her.

"It's a start, anyway. At least he won't have to stand on tiptoe to kiss me good night."

Alison laughed, although she did feel sorry for her friend because she was so embarrassed about her height.

"I'm doing a piece for the newspaper on new couples on campus. Can I include you two?" Julie asked mischievously. Another of Julie's interests was writing.

"Don't you dare. At least not yet," Heather instructed. "We aren't an official *couple* yet. I mean I just told *you* girls about it, don't go telling the world."

"Did you find your radiator, Grease?" That was Julie's nickname for Alison. Both girls teased her about her interest in cars—

especially when she would join a group of boys at a party and talk about nothing else.

"Yes. I found a nearly new one at the junkyard for twenty-five dollars. I'm really excited about it."

"It's almost as exciting as my date," Heather said and giggled.

"In a different category, I think. I'm putting it in this weekend with a boy I met at the junkyard."

Both girls' eyes widened in curiosity. "Who?" they asked as a chorus.

"I've never seen him before. He must go to another school," Alison replied quickly, knowing they were trying to picture who he was. She didn't want to tell them too much just yet—the coincidences surrounding their meeting; the little somersault of her heart—it was still too soon to be talked about. "I'm helping him put in an engine this weekend, too."

"Wow. Just like that?" Heather asked.

"He's easy to talk to. A nice guy," Alison found herself saying defensively.

"Is this one of those love-at-first-sight things?" Julie wanted to know.

"What did I tell you yesterday, Al? This is your mysterious visitor," Heather cried jubilantly, clapping her hands. "It's amazing."

"OK, you guys. There is no love involved—except for maybe a love of grease and getting cars running," Alison told them loftily and was glad the night was dark so they couldn't see her blush. "I've never put in an engine, and although that sounds incredibly boring to you, it's not to me. It's going to be fun."

"Yeah, I suppose it will be. You were going to put in an engine with—" Julie stopped in mid-sentence. "Gee, sorry, Al."

"It's OK. I know—with Marty," Alison finished for her. "It'll be good for me. Even you guys would probably order some cure like that for me."

"Yeah, you're right. Except that it's not the sort of activity that we think of first," Heather added practically.

"Hey, Al, what's this guy's name?" Julie asked.

"Billy—Billy Kendall."

Alison thought his name had a nice ring to it when she said it out loud, but she didn't mention anything more to her friends. Her thoughts of Billy were brushed away as they pulled into the parking lot of the movie theater.

In the deli where they stopped on the way

home, the three girls studied the patrons as though they were characters in the spy thriller they had just seen.

Julie hunched down in the booth, narrowing her eyes to slits.

"Julie, you look crazy," Alison said, giggling. "Before you know it, someone's going to arrest you for escaping the loony bin."

"The question is—is that man in the denim jacket involved in some Mafia scheme?" Julie asked with a mock French accent.

"Actually, I think this restaurant is a Mafia front. Look at how suspicious the waiters act," observed Heather. "They seem anxious to get us out of here."

"I wonder why," said Alison. "Could it be that we're taking up the space of full-paying customers and only ordered Cokes?"

"You *would* think of that." Julie shook her head. "What are you, a double agent or something?"

Alison got up to leave. "C'mon. Let's go see if there's some food at my place."

Sure enough, there were a couple of apple pies cooling on the counter when they walked in.

Alison considered herself pretty lucky.

She loved her home—it was unusual, but it suited her family so well. She liked how it could be a very private place, but at the same time it offered room for many people.

Her friends loved it for their own reasons. Julie's parents were divorced, so that meant she spent only every other weekend with her father and the rest of the time with her mom. The inn was solid and welcoming for her. Heather was the oldest in a family of six kids, and she loved the peace and adult atmosphere of Alison's home.

"I can come over and not worry about tripping over a toy or finding a banana peel under the rug," she explained.

"My dad wants to know if you'll work this weekend," Alison asked Heather while she cut a pie.

"Sure," Heather replied. "While you're off putting in an engine?"

"Yes."

"Hey, Al, you never told us what this mysterious Billy Kendall looks like. His name sounds awfully familiar."

"Probably because it's so common," Alison guessed. "He's got red hair and freckles and is kind of cute."

The girls laughed. "Any other distinguishing qualities?"

"Well, he's got a great smile, a soft way of speaking, and he's just comfortable. That's all I can say."

Heather and Julie exchanged glances. "That, my dear, is a pretty good start," Heather announced dramatically.

"We can see already that he doesn't blend into the woodwork," added Julie.

"Oh, you say that about all boys."

Heather took a large bite of pie. "Mmmm, great. By the way, did you sign up for the float committee, Al?"

"Yes. When do we get together?"

"In about a week."

The float committee had been formed to decorate the "royal float" for the May Day parade. It had to be set up so that there was a special throne for the May Day queen and her court. This year the junior class was in charge of it. Alison had signed up to work on the committee because she wanted to keep herself busy. It was one thing her friends had insisted on after Marty had died, and she hadn't stopped since then. Now, she was starting to enjoy class activities and looked forward to the float.

Alison shook her head at the thought. "What would I do without my social directors?"

Julie held up her hands. "Who knows, my friend!" she exclaimed.

Heather winked. "You know, Julie, I'm not sure we're needed anymore. She seems to be managing quite well by herself these days. Soon we might let her out on her own."

"On a leash," Julie added, and the girls burst into hysterical laughter.

Chapter Four

"**I** didn't realize your family ran an inn, Alison," Billy said when he phoned early the next morning.

At the sound of his voice, Alison felt her breath catch in her throat. It was like jumping off the high dive or flipping on a trampoline.

"You'll have to see it," she replied.

"I will, when I pick you up. I've already got the engine so I'll be there in fifteen minutes, around ten. OK?"

"OK, see you soon." Alison's heart was beating quickly as she hung up the phone.

Alison settled into the torn seat of the truck. It was the same pickup that had pulled up beside her the other evening. She wondered if he knew it had been she on the road.

"What school do you go to?" she asked, watching him mash the blue and white cap down over his forehead.

It felt strange and a little awkward finding out bits of information about a new person. Alison had always known all there was to know about Marty; so there was never any need to ask all these silly questions.

"I go to Bradley. And you must go to Lee."

She smiled and nodded.

"First, we're going to the car wash to clean the grunge off the engine," Billy said, winking at her.

Alison was struck again by the ease that she felt with Billy. One phone conversation and a meeting at a junkyard were hardly grounds for friendship, yet she experienced an unmistakable warmth when she was with him.

Billy pulled into the car wash and jumped out of the truck. His springy energy caused Alison's heart to take a small leap—as if she expected him to hop away.

She got out, too. "I can help or watch," she said.

"Watching's help," Billy said, dropping the gate on the pickup to hose down the engine. "Of course, you should expect to get dirty, but that comes later. No need to be unrecognizable yet."

Alison laughed. "Is that grease already?"

She pointed to the bluish-black smudge on his forehead.

"No. That's a bruise I got yesterday, fooling around," he said quickly, but abruptly his expression turned mischievous. "Have you been swimming yet this year, Alison?" he asked with mock innocence.

Before she could reply, he turned the hose on her.

"Billy!"

Alison looked down at her drenched T-shirt. The purple ribbon she'd used to tie her hair back clung to it like a dead snake.

"Couldn't resist," Billy said, chuckling. "I knew you'd look so cute."

"Wet is a better description." She couldn't stop herself from bursting into laughter. "Do I spend the rest of the day squelching around in these sneakers?"

"No. I'll lend you some dry ones, although they might not be as fancy as those you're wearing."

They both looked down at Alison's old ripped shoes and started laughing. Absently Billy handed her the hose. She took the opportunity to give him a dose of his own medicine.

"Ahhh!" Billy tried to ward off the blast of water with his arms. His hair formed damp

31

ringlets across his forehead, and when he looked at Alison, his eyes were bright. "I deserved that, didn't I?"

"Afraid so. You look cute," she added, mimicking him. He made a face at her.

"Let's stop for doughnuts, and then we've got to get to work. Did I tell you I work part-time at Whoppin' Donuts?"

"No. Do you get a discount?"

"Yeah—on day-olds."

Billy hopped into the truck, dripping water over the seat and the floor. The two of them giggled so hard on the way to his house that he could barely keep his eyes on the road.

Billy's house was a brown clapboard with a sun deck extending from one side. It was located near one of Lenox's old abandoned estates.

"I used to play over there as a kid," he told Alison, pointing out the stone gateposts that marked the estate driveway.

"My parents looked at some of these estates when they wanted to buy an inn," said Alison. "But most of them are too big."

"They're not good for anything these days, and definitely too expensive and too big to live in."

When Billy opened the garage door, Alison

saw the other truck, which needed the new engine. She also saw two motorcycles, one bigger than the other. Fresh mud was trapped in the tire treads; so she guessed they'd been ridden recently. She remembered Billy had mentioned needing to overhaul his engine so he could transport bikes.

"Those are yours?" she asked.

"Yeah. Both of them," he said. He got out the come-a-long and hooked it onto the elm tree branch that hung over the driveway. "OK, now we'll push my truck up to the tree so that the engine's underneath the come-a-long."

The come-a-long was essential to their work. It was a sort of pulley contraption that Alison had seen before but had never used. They had to hook it to the old engine in order to remove it, and then they would use it again to lower the new engine in place.

"Now we've got to disconnect the radiator hoses," Billy said.

At the mention of the radiator, Alison was reminded of her date with Jeff. *What a creep compared to Billy,* she thought as Billy's expert hands moved confidently in the machine.

"Hey," Alison said out loud as she put a bucket under the truck to catch the drainage from the radiator. "The night before we met at the junkyard, I was walking on Old Mill Road. Was that you who stopped and asked me if I needed a ride?"

Billy looked up, leaning his elbows on the side of the truck. "That was you?" he asked, then hooted. "When I saw you in the junkyard, I thought your profile looked familiar, but I wasn't sure enough to say anything."

Alison went on to explain just why she had been walking at that hour. She left out the part about how she had almost accepted a ride from him, just telling him how mad she had been at Jeff. "You're different," she concluded, all of a sudden feeling shy. "You don't seem threatened because a girl knows about cars."

Alison hadn't really planned on telling Billy all the details, but the words had come so easily. She felt good telling him what she thought. Billy seemed to like the story, and he laughed at the image of Jeff's bumbling under the hood of a car.

Standing on either side of the truck, they were disconnecting the electrical wires now.

"And next"—Billy flipped his wrench in the air and caught it with the same hand—

"we're going to unbolt the engine from the bell housing."

Alison struggled with a sticky bolt that seemed to be rusted in place. She remembered how Marty used to call her "Jell-O-wrists" because she could barely turn bolts that he could undo in a second.

"Are you one of those people who has trouble with mayonnaise jar lids?" Billy asked, noticing her concentrated effort.

"No," she said. "I'll get it—see?" With one final thrust the bolt moved.

"Bravo. Next step—unbolting the motor mounts. But first, let's have some lunch. Mom and Dad are out for the day; so I'll have to make it."

Hours had flown by, but at the mention of lunch Alison realized that she had worked up an appetite. She poured lemonade while Billy made fantastic hero sandwiches on onion rolls. The kitchen was wide, filled with hanging copper pans and pots. It opened into a spacious dining area, where they sat down for lunch.

"I can't get over it. I've never worked on cars with a girl before," Billy remarked after they had finished the heroes. "You're really good."

"Don't tell me you're a macho-Jeff under-neath the surface," Alison said, knowing it was far from the truth. "As for me, I've never eaten such a good hero sandwich."

"Are you suggesting we've got a case of role reversal here?"

She shrugged. "I just don't like to be put in a box. People shouldn't be so strict about what boys can do and what girls can do. It has more to do with what you're capable of."

"Well said," he added and grinned. "Here, try one of my chocolate-chip cookies. I made them especially for you." He handed her a plastic container.

Alison viewed him with surprise. She wondered at his last remark. Had he looked forward to this day as much as she had? She masked her surprise by replying, "You *are* domestic, aren't you?"

"Try to be." Billy winked at her. "But I still have my wild side."

Intrigued by that comment, Alison fol-lowed Billy out to the driveway. It was time to get back to work.

Under his direction, she helped bolt a chain to the sides of the engine; the chain was then hooked to the come-a-long.

"OK, grab the other side of the chain,

Alison. We're pulling it forward now, off the bell housing shaft. That's it—great. Now let's pull it up."

"It's swinging!" Alison cried as the heavy engine started swaying out of control above the truck.

"OK, OK." They both strained to steady the engine. "Easy. Now there, we've got it." Billy wiped the back of his arm along his sweaty brow, leaving a streak of oil. "Whew. Let's dump this and quit. Tomorrow, it's this same process, only we put the new one in."

As they washed up at the outside faucet, Alison asked, "Do you want to come over and take a tour of the inn?"

Billy nodded. "Yeah, sounds great. Can I take a quick shower first?"

Alison wandered around the garage while she waited for him, noting that one whole section of the workbench was filled with parts for motorcycles. She guessed they were dirt bikes. Marty had once thought about racing dirt bikes. Billy looked like the kind of guy who would own them just for fun. There were plenty of trails through the woods to ride on, she thought, poking at a curl of dried mud on one of the tires.

*   *   *

"Pleased to meet you." Alison's father shook Billy's hand firmly. "How's the truck going?"

"We're making progress," Billy said. "Alison's a great worker."

"We never thought she'd turn out to be a mechanic," her father said and chuckled.

"She does have strange interests, but you get used to her after a while," her mother put in jokingly.

"Mother!" Alison groaned in embarrassment.

Billy looked up at the beamed ceiling. "This is a great house. How old is it?"

"About a hundred and fifty years," Mr. Matlock said.

"Let me give you the guided tour that I promised," Alison suggested, touching Billy's arm lightly.

He grinned at her. "I've seen this place from the road so many times and always wondered what it was like inside."

"Actually, we live in a small part of the house," Alison explained, leading the way through the monstrous kitchen, which was equipped like that of a small restaurant. Then she showed him the sitting room, decorated with Persian rugs, antiques, and a grand piano.

"I love the stone fireplace," Billy said. "Wouldn't it be fun to curl up next to it on a cold winter's night?"

"It is—with hot chocolate." Alison's gaze met his, then she moved quickly ahead of him toward her room. "And this is my hangout."

Billy walked quietly from one wall to the next, surveying Alison's collection of pictures. His eyes settled on a group of trophies on the bookcase. "These were Marty's?" he asked quietly.

"Yes."

"The guy was a star, wasn't he?" Billy fingered a gold trophy, then moved on to a photo of Marty's silver racer.

"He was." Alison's throat tightened, and she swallowed hard. She glanced out the window at the garden, which was now full of daffodils.

"I had a good time with you today, Alison," Billy commented, coming up behind her.

She could feel his breath at the back of her neck, ruffling her hair. "Me, too. It was fun," she told him, without turning around.

"You're a great mechanic."

She laughed. "So are you."

"It might be too early to tell, but I think we make a good team."

"Maybe." A blush crept into Alison's cheeks.

She led him out through the bar, where a few guests were gathered. At the door Billy turned to her. "I'll be by for you tomorrow morning at nine, OK?"

"OK."

"You've got grease on your face." Affectionately he rubbed her cheek with his thumb, then turned toward the driveway.

Alison watched him walk toward his father's truck, her hand on the cheek he had just touched.

The process of putting in the new engine was simply the same as taking the old one out, in reverse. The engine had to be lowered from the elm tree toward the truck cavity, then pushed toward the bell housing and carefully placed in. The difficult part was keeping the engine straight and not allowing it to sway.

When they finally had it in place and were busy bolting in the parts, Billy said, "You're a lot of fun to work with, Alison. You sure you never did this before—with Marty?"

"No, we never put in an engine. We were going to . . ." She explained about the accident.

"Sorry—didn't mean to bring up a bad memory." He studied her for a moment, ready for her tears.

"Billy, I'm not an eggshell. I won't break if you talk about Marty. It's been a year, and I'm used to him not being around. Of course, I miss him. We grew up together. He was my first boyfriend." She shrugged, not entirely satisfied that she had convinced him that she could handle herself.

"OK. But I guess I expected you to be more sensitive, you know, burst into tears or something if I said the wrong thing. You're not like that, I'm beginning to see." His gaze met hers, and Alison's heart wavered.

He cleared his throat. "We can work on your radiator tomorrow after school if you like."

"OK. Let's see how the engine works." She got in the driver's seat and started it.

Billy cheered as the engine roared to life.

Billy's parents invited Alison to stay for dinner. After dinner Billy drove her home. It was one of those balmy spring nights with a full moon that casts a yellow glow over the

41

road. Alison sat close to Billy, while he concentrated on the smooth purr of his new engine.

"Sounds good, Billy," Alison said, feeling pleased that she was part of its success.

"Doesn't it?" Billy's hand closed over hers. She was filled with warmth at his touch. He started singing an old song she hadn't heard in years, and she hummed along, harmonizing.

Alison felt so good with him that she was disappointed when the pickup pulled into her driveway.

As she started to get out of the truck, Billy leaned over, and Alison thought he was going to kiss her. Instead, he tickled her. She doubled over, laughing, and ran to the front door.

That night, as she lay in bed, Billy's face filled her thoughts, and his laughter rang in her ears. She pored over every detail of the day as though each were a treasure. She felt as though the rusty bolts in her head had suddenly been loosened and freed.

Chapter Five

"So how'd your weekend go?" Heather asked anxiously Monday morning as the three girls piled into Julie's car.

"Great. We're doing my radiator after school," Alison informed her friends.

Julie shrieked. "That's not the answer we're expecting, Al! Something romantic, please."

"I never meant to be attracted to Billy," Alison reflected dreamily. The truth was, she hadn't thought of anything but Billy all weekend. She kept rolling his image around in her mind. Now she was remembering his brown eyes meeting hers in that mischievous way of his—as though a joke were on the tip of his tongue. She realized how she'd been drawn to him from the first day she saw that red hair.

"Do you think you and Billy are up for inclusion in my article on campus couples?" Julie wanted to know as she swung into the school parking lot. "Nearly everyone in school has been dating the same person for eons, and we need new blood."

Lee High School was a box-shaped brick structure surrounded by a sweeping lawn. The tennis courts, pool, and gyms were hidden behind a row of birch trees.

"She sounds like a vampire, doesn't she?" Heather said, joking.

"You know how popular these articles are," Julie went on, ignoring Heather. "But I'm so desperate for material that I'm ready to make something up."

"How about making up an interview with Mick Jagger?" Heather suggested.

"You guys are a great help." Julie sighed. "We still want to know about your weekend, Al."

"I was hoping you'd forgotten," Alison said and grinned. "But if you have to know: first, we went to the car wash to clean the engine Billy bought for his truck—"

Both girls groaned.

"Spare us the grimy details, Grease," Heather complained.

"What we really want to know is, did he kiss you?" Julie asked bluntly.

"No—we don't know each other that well,

Julie. Aren't you rushing things?" Alison felt hot with embarrassment. Just the thought of kissing Billy made her very warm.

"Just trying to see how far this relationship has progressed."

"Yes, well, knowing that whatever I say may end up in the school newspaper makes me a little nervous," Alison told her, hoisting a stack of books under one arm. "I've got to run—I've got PE first period. Catch you later."

"Real cute getaway, Al," Heather called after her. "See you."

Alison ran toward the gym. She knew she wouldn't be able to avoid her friends' curiosity about Billy much longer. They were hot on her tail to know all the details, and she couldn't blame them. The fact that Billy went to another school meant that they were doubly curious. The usual channels of gossip couldn't touch Billy and Alison because no one could observe them together during the day.

The weekend with Billy stood out in Alison's mind as something special. Neither of her friends could understand what it was like to grow close to somebody while putting in an engine. Of course, they knew all about her relationship with Marty, but there had been few surprises with him. She and Marty had been buddies long before they became romantically involved, and then the romance was so slow moving that Alison wasn't quite sure when it had begun. There had been no anniversary and no particular day or event that stood out in her mind. . . .

And just why was she thinking this way? She remembered how Billy had looked, leaning toward her, and wondered if he was thinking about kissing her. She tried to imagine what his lips would feel like, his arms closing around her back, and she trembled.

Billy and Alison had put in her radiator that evening. They tested her car by driving to a cafe.

"When I first saw you at the junkyard, I didn't expect that you'd be like you are," Billy told Alison. They had chosen a corner table where they were away from the bustle and glaring lights. Soft music cushioned the room.

"What did you expect?" Alison questioned, spooning the whipped cream off the top of her cocoa. That night her heart almost stopped in anticipation. She couldn't imagine what he would say next, and everything he said seemed so meaningful.

"You're different. I mean, most of the girls I know who work on cars aren't as pretty as you," he said, his blush deepening.

"That could be a sexist remark, Billy." Alison pretended to frown.

"I didn't mean it that way. I just meant, we seem to get along well. I don't want to get together only when we need to fix a car."

Alison laughed. "Yeah—I do like to do other things."

"Like dance?" Billy grinned, offering her his hand.

"Sure."

They danced slowly to a melancholy love song. They were the only couple dancing, but it didn't matter to Alison. She closed her eyes and enjoyed the tingling warmth of Billy's hand on the small of her back, guiding her movements. She rested her cheek on his red-checkered shirt and breathed in the mingled scents of cologne and motor oil, memorizing the way he felt next to her. His breath against her ear sent tremors down her spine, and she wanted the moment to last forever.

When the song was over, Billy led Alison back to their table, his arm dropping to her waist.

"We'd better get home," he said, checking

his watch. "You said you had to be back by eleven."

"You don't want to risk my turning into a pumpkin," she quipped.

"Or worse, your car."

Billy and Alison walked out to her car, and Billy climbed into the passenger seat. He stroked her hair as she started the car. "Your hair is so pretty—like a waterfall," he murmured, smiling at her in the dark.

Alison didn't know what to say; she was glad she was driving so she could stare straight ahead. Marty hadn't complimented her very often, and she felt shy and awkward now. She supposed that with Marty a lot had been taken for granted, even though they were devoted to each other.

"Have you gone out much since Marty died?" Billy asked suddenly.

"Do you mean, 'out' as in leaving the house or as in dating?"

"As in dating."

"No. But my friends have kept me from sitting home. For a while they fixed me up with anyone they could find, just to keep me busy. It got to be embarrassing, though. Nobody likes a set-up."

"I would have," he said quietly, "if it had been with you."

For the rest of the ride, he kept his hand resting lightly on the back of her neck. She turned the car into her driveway so Billy could pick up his truck.

Knowing that she wanted him to kiss her, Alison cleared her throat, remained seated, and kept both hands on the steering wheel. "Thanks for helping me with my car," she said.

"You're welcome." Then Billy touched her hair again and pulled her gently toward him, covering her lips with his. Alison melted at his touch—she might have been a snowflake disappearing against warm skin.

"I like everything I know about you, Alison Matlock," Billy whispered into her hair, and she smiled.

"Will I see you this week?" she asked, not wanting the day or the magic to end.

"How about Saturday? This week I have to work Tuesday, Wednesday, and Thursday, and I've got to spend some time catching up on my classes. And on Friday I've—got other plans. But Saturday would be great."

Alison looked up and smiled. Again, his mouth met hers. She was caught up in the power of his kiss surging over her, making her feel suddenly reckless. It felt good to let go a little bit after a year of thinking about someone who would never kiss her again. Now Alison wanted to experience Billy, let herself feel what she hadn't been able to feel in a long time. . . .

"I can tell by the look in your eyes that you've kissed him," Julie announced triumphantly.

The three girls were sitting in Julie's bedroom on Friday afternoon. Her house was actually a converted barn, and Julie's room was a loft, reached by a spiral staircase.

"Julie, you make me feel like I have to keep my love life under lock and key." Alison sighed. Although she had told her friends about her date with Billy Monday night, she hadn't told them about his kissing her; she wasn't ready to talk about it.

Julie handed her a plate of chocolate cupcakes. "I promise I won't take notes. Come on, I'm almost done with that article, anyway. You can trust Jules."

Yes, Alison could trust her. Sometimes she trusted her friends more than she trusted herself.

After Billy had driven off on Monday

night, Alison's head started swirling. It wasn't just the dizziness caused by their first kiss that sent her reeling—something was nagging at her. Part of it was the memory of Marty. She knew she couldn't remain faithful to Marty forever, but she felt a little guilty about how quickly she had fallen for Billy. When she had gone into her room, she had taken Marty's picture and stared at it for a long time, trying to sort out her thoughts.

She was also bothered by a slight feeling of dread, as though she were afraid of falling in love again. The pain that she had felt from Marty's death made her never want to get that close to anyone ever again, just in case he would leave her empty, too.

Julie's curiosity didn't help either, even though Alison knew that her friend would probably be able to sort through her mess in a second. She had that kind of mind. It was still too soon to talk about it, though. Alison wouldn't even know where to begin explaining the chaos that she felt.

Julie broke through and interrupted her deep thoughts. "Hey, Ted told me that there's a big motocross race today; in fact, right now. His friend Steve is competing." Ted was her brother, who was home from college for spring vacation. He had been heavily involved in motorcycles when he was in high school. "Shall we go and see what it's like?"

Alison frowned. She still felt queasy just thinking about races. Julie was looking steadily at her, trying to determine whether she should talk Alison into going.

"Come on, Al. It'll be fun. Besides, it's only dirt bikes. You won't know any of the riders. It may even be good for you." Julie's practical mind was persuasive, and Alison started to think about the excitement of a race. She remembered how few things gave her the same thrill as a good race.

Maybe Julie was right—because it was motorcycles and not cars, it wouldn't be scary or upsetting to her. It would just be exciting, like the old days. Maybe now was the time to face some of her fears—Billy had already taught her that much. She had to go on living.

She took a deep breath. "Sure, I'll go," she finally said. Julie silently took her shoulder and gave her a good squeeze.

Chapter Six

Sandwiched between Julie and Heather, with Ted next to Julie, Alison absorbed the sights and sounds of the track.

The motocross track was different from what Alison was used to with stock-car racing. The dirt track was covered with S-curves and hills, sometimes one after another. Ted said they were called whoop-de-dos.

"There's Steve!" Ted exclaimed, pointing to the mass of bikers below. "Number twenty-eight."

Alison picked him out, hunched close to his handlebars, headed for the slotted gate, where each bike waited for the starting signal.

When the gates opened, the bikes sprang forward, spewing trails of dirt from their rear wheels.

"It's just a two-lap race," Ted explained, before he turned his attention to the track. It was obvious nobody would get much more information from him until the race was over.

The bikes churned and plowed up the hills, some of them tipping over, the riders struggling to right themselves. Mechanics rushed on and off the track, helping those who had engine trouble or had to be pulled out of the stream of oncoming bikes.

Alison watched as gloved hands twisted throttles on handlebars, expertly sending the bikes around the bends and over the curves. One in particular, number eighty-one, had a familiar stance. She was instantly reminded of Marty. But why? There was no reason to think of him now, here, unless it was just being at the track that triggered the memory.

"How're you doing, Alison?" Heather shouted above the din.

"Fine, just fine." Actually, Alison was pleased with how well she was holding up. She was under control, not the trembly, nervous person she thought she might be at a track. Maybe it was Billy's influence, she thought, smiling to herself. He had changed her life a little, just in the short time they'd known each other. He was special.

"I knew it would be good for you to see this race, Al," Julie said, not taking her eyes from the track. "I mean, it's not so dangerous. Steve is a real pro. The more professional someone is, the less chance there is of getting hurt."

"I know."

"Oh, sure, I know you know. I forgot." She looked apologetic.

"Steve's moving up front. Look—he's closing in on the leader!"

"Who's that lead bike? Number eighty-one?"

"He's holding position really well."

"Oh, no—look!" Alison jumped to her feet. A rider had been flipped off his bike: the scene before her revived old images of another accident. The rider lay on the track in the path of flying bikes, and one landed on him. Medics rushed over the fence toward the fallen rider, and somewhere an ambulance screamed to life.

"No, Alison—don't look." Heather's fingers pressed into her upper arm, pulling her back to her seat.

"About three people get pulled off the track with injuries every meet," Ted announced casually. "It's really a safe sport."

"You can say both those things in the

same breath?" Alison questioned, but Ted wasn't listening.

The driver was heaped onto a stretcher. Alison wondered if he had a girlfriend. It would be better if he didn't, she thought. She was very relieved she didn't know any of the riders.

A few minutes later, Ted, Julie, and Heather jumped up and screamed as Steve tore through the finish, taking second place.

"I'm going down to congratulate him," Ted said, hugging everyone he knew along the way down the bleachers.

"C'mon, Alison," Julie said and followed her brother. "Let's go congratulate Steve. He's been dying to meet you ever since I told him you used to go with Marty."

Alison knew Steve had a case of hero worship where Marty was concerned. She wished she could tell him not to. She wanted to say, "Go idolize a rock star or a baseball player— not Marty. It might be dangerous to your health."

Yet Alison knew she couldn't do that. The minute she met Steve she realized he had his heart set on racing. He was a fresh-faced, gangly boy with buckteeth and a wide grin. His expression was jubilant.

"Congratulations, Steve. I've heard a lot about you," Alison told him.

"Yeah? Really? Well, I think I've heard more about you, and Marty Willins. I mean . . ." He blushed, obviously at a loss for words.

Alison saved him from embarrassment. "It's OK. I'm used to it by now. Marty was a great racer, but that was cars. You're showing great promise on bikes."

"Thanks. Coming from you, that's a compliment." He shook her hand vigorously. "Well, I've got to go. The mechanic's checking my bike out now."

"Good luck—though you don't seem to need it."

"I think that, besides taking second in that heat, meeting you made his day," Heather said.

They settled down to watch the next heat in which Steve was entered. The bikes bucked out of the gate as before. Dirt and gravel crackled under the tires. The roar of the crowd caused Alison's skin to rise up in goose bumps. Why was it that the excitement thrilled through her veins even though she was scared? What was it about racing that so absorbed her? It seemed crazy; yet she reminded herself that she had loved racing before it took Marty away.

She saw Steve roaring along the outside, catching up to number eighty-one, whom she had not really watched during the first heat. An S-curve put number eighty-one in front, and the rider took a series of hills with relative ease, rising off the seat, crouching over his bike in perfect form. The other riders tried to follow his lead.

"Look how he takes those whoop-de-dos," Ted said admiringly.

"Steve's moving in on number eighty-one, isn't he? Who is that rider?" Alison asked.

"I don't know. But he rode a different bike in the first heat."

Alison listened to this conversation with one ear, her mind and body tuned into the engines' roar, the flying dirt, the well-timed movements of the riders before her.

Then Steve dropped back, his bike falling over on an S-curve. Number eighty-one surged ahead. Steve struggled up from under his bike, and a mechanic helped him move to the side of the track.

"What a bummer!" Ted wailed.

Number eighty-one skidded across the finish. The checkered flag came down with a fluttery swoop. The crowd's cheers accompanied the roar of the following bikes.

Wondering about poor Steve, Alison asked, "What happened to Steve?"

"He's OK. Looks like he'll finish about tenth," reported Ted, pointing him out. Sure enough, Steve had joined the other riders, whose cycles screamed past the finish line.

Alison's gaze then fell on the winner's circle. The bright yellow bike was straddled by a boy in a blue and gold driving suit. He was watching his points tallied while fans congratulated him. Then he turned toward the crowd and yanked off his helmet.

For a moment Alison's heart seemed to stop beating. She heard herself gasp as the familiar red hair tumbled out from under the helmet. "Billy!" The unmistakable, triumphant grin that had gotten her attention at the junkyard now filled her with a gripping fear.

"Billy," she whispered again, oblivious to everyone around her.

"That's Billy Kendall?" Julie and Heather said in chorus.

"That's him, all right," Ted informed them excitedly. "One of the best riders you'll ever see. You should see all his trophies."

Billy's face blurred before Alison's eyes.

"I didn't know," she mumbled, stumbling down the bleachers and away from the dusty track and the bikes. She wanted to be as far away from the heady, intoxicating wave of triumph as she could get.

Chapter Seven

"Alison, wait up!"

Heather raced along the planked bleachers, trying to catch up to Alison. "Alison!"

"For crying out loud, stop, will you?" Julie puffed along, bringing up the rear.

Alison stopped below the bleachers and turned to face them.

"You didn't know Billy raced motocross?" Heather took her friend by the shoulders and stared into her sorrowful eyes, immediately knowing the answer to her question. "He should have told you, Al."

"Maybe he knew how you would react," Julie guessed.

"It's not fair, though. He should've said something. Given me some warning, you know." Alison was choking back tears.

"Yes, but how was he supposed to tell you? You wouldn't want anything to do with

61

him if you knew. He didn't want to take that chance, I bet."

"So he didn't bother to think about what the deception might do to me?" she demanded. "Doesn't he know what I've been through?"

"Sure, he understands, but this isn't the same thing. Marty had a freak accident. You know yourself, it's rare that people are killed in stock-car races."

"People still get hurt," Alison insisted and kicked at the dirt in anger.

"People get hurt lots of ways, Al. You can slip in the shower and break your neck," Julie said.

"The question is, Al, can you go on with this relationship?" Heather asked philosophically.

"Sounds like a question from a women's magazine article," Alison said bitterly.

"It's a question you've got to ask, Al," Julie put in. "You've gone through one bad scene with Marty. Chances are slim that you'd have a repeat performance with Billy, but it might be too hard to handle if you did."

"Don't you think I realize that? I thought I did a good job of shielding myself from being hurt again—up until now."

"You did. But you can't predict being attracted to somebody," Heather said.

"Yes, I wish I had a crystal ball," Alison lamented.

"Well, it wouldn't do any good," insisted Julie. "Come on, let's get a Coke and talk about this some more."

They bought Cokes at the concession stand. Alison sipped hers without tasting it. If only Billy weren't into racing, it would be so easy. Why hadn't he said something?

"Alison?"

The surprised voice belonged to Billy. The three girls turned around.

"Oh, you must be Billy," Heather remarked.

"That's right, and you must be—?"

Alison suddenly realized she hadn't told Billy too much about her friends. Julie helped her through the introductions.

"Congratulations," Heather and Julie said together.

"Thanks." Billy grinned and winked at Alison. She managed a small smile.

"Well, we're going to watch Steve in the next race," Heather said. "Nice to meet you, Billy."

"Same here."

The girls walked away, leaving Alison and Billy alone. Alison knew she was staring at him, her eyes shimmering with unshed tears. She didn't want to speak, but her words came tumbling out: "You didn't tell me you raced."

"Would it have made a difference?" he asked softly, stroking her cold, trembling hand.

"I might not have gotten to know you so well."

"That would have been a shame." He smiled, lifting her chin so that her eyes met his. "Can't you guess why I didn't tell you?"

"Yes, but I think it was unfair, under the circumstances. You should've told me," she said in an injured tone.

"Sorry. I didn't mean to hurt you." Billy kicked a rock across the dirt, and Alison watched until it stopped at the root of a poplar tree.

"Did you always hate racing so much, Alison?" Billy asked.

She felt suddenly distant from Billy, set apart from the whole scene, as if she were watching it from the top of the bleachers. The two experiences, Marty and now Billy, hung together in her mind, and there seemed to be no way of separating them. "I used to love racing. I loved it so much," she said. Then she focused on Billy. "I was enjoying the race today, until I found out that you were in it," she admitted.

"I understand," Billy told her regretfully. "But you have to understand me, too."

If Billy only knew the nightmares that she had. She challenged him. "Have you ever lost anyone in a race?"

"No, but I've seen plenty of accidents. Everybody gets up and rides again. Once in a while somebody gets badly hurt, but it's usually from inexperience or foolishness. It's no big deal. This isn't considered a dangerous sport, you know."

"That's what everyone said about stock-car racing."

"I'm not going to argue with you. You're not someone I'd try to convince, Alison. You're speaking from a different experience. But from the driver's seat, it doesn't look bad." Billy's eyebrows rose as if he were asking for Alison's approval.

"I hope it never is bad for you, Billy," Alison told him.

"It won't be." He was so confident, so sunny. *Just like Marty*, she reflected. *Marty would've said something like that.* She felt suddenly chilled.

"Are we still going out tomorrow?" Billy asked as though he'd been reading her thoughts.

Alison wished she'd never met Billy. She wished she could roll back her life and start over. But Billy had jumped into her heart.

It hurt to talk to him like this—it hurt to talk to him at all. "I don't think so, Billy. I'll see you, OK?" she said, her voice quivering. She started to turn away.

He wasn't easily put off, and he grabbed her arm. "Is that a 'seeya' as in, 'seeya today or tomorrow,' or as in 'I don't want to seeya anymore'?"

Alison tried for something in between, something neutral. "I don't want to see you for a bit, please."

"For real?" He looked stunned, hurt. His eyes didn't have a trace of their usual gleam.

Her heart ached. "For real. I need to think, Billy." She scarcely recognized her own voice.

He shrugged, managing a half-smile. "Think happy," he said almost as a question.

She turned and left him standing alone, knowing that to watch him walk away from her would be more painful. She told herself she could forget him. She could forget all about him and get back to that safe place she was in before she met him.

"You're not going to forget him—zap—like that," Heather announced emphatically. "You can't go backward, Alison."

Julie, Heather, and Alison were making flowers for the May Day float. Alison twisted a length of green crepe paper around a pipe cleaner to make a stem.

"Sure I can, Heather," she insisted. "Come on, I've only known Billy a short time. We don't have a history like Marty and I had."

Heather reached for more pipe cleaners.

Heather's room was done in lavender and blue. The carpeting was a luscious, thick blue pile that you could sink your toes into. Along one wall was a ballet bar and mirror for dance practice.

Julie, ever conscious of her weight, sucked in her stomach in front of the mirror. She was on another diet.

"The thing is, he didn't try to hurt you on purpose, Al. It looks to me like he's been trying to protect you from getting upset," she said.

"He didn't do me any favors," Alison replied. "Besides, I think it makes a lot more sense for me to get out of this before I fall in love with Billy."

"Before? Aren't you in love already?" Heather questioned, her eyes zeroing in on Alison.

"Of course not," Alison snapped in denial.

"I suppose it depends on what your definition of 'love' is," Julie put in. "I think sometimes it's good to write a list to see if you *are* in love. You know, an examination of your feelings. I mean, people are all different. For example, from my interviews, I've found that some people can't eat when they're in love. Woody Allen gets nauseous when he falls in love."

"I didn't know you interviewed Woody Allen," Alison said, giggling. "Look, I'm not nauseous, I eat fine, and I know I'm not in love. It doesn't feel like it did with Marty."

But she remembered Billy's kiss. The heat of it had lingered on her lips, warming her for a long time afterward. It was unlike any kiss she had ever had—even from Marty.

"That's because you're more mature," Heather insisted sagely. "Love matures, people mature—"

"I just love the way you two have analyzed my condition. I really think you should go into business—J. Merritt and H. Chadwick, Psychologists," Alison interrupted.

"We're not often wrong. Mark my words—you, Alison Matlock, are already in love." Heather stated this with utmost confidence.

Alison's paper flower trembled on the end of its pipe cleaner stalk. She fiddled with its petals, trying to make it look at least partly real.

"No, I'm not," Alison retorted, realizing that she sounded like a pouting child. Heather and Julie exchanged glances.

"The question is, Al, can you handle it?" Heather got to the heart of the matter.

Alison shivered. Her friends really knew her well. No, she knew she couldn't handle it. Suddenly she felt awfully frail.

"I'm not prepared to lose two people. I think it's over between Billy and me," she said slowly and quietly. But she was already miserable with her decision.

Alison was grateful for a busy week. She ran around arranging details for the float committee and studied for two tests. She didn't have to think about what was lying just under the surface of her mind.

After her conversation with Heather and

Julie, she had realized that she couldn't live with the fear she felt whenever she thought of Billy racing. It was too much.

She also knew that she couldn't demand that Billy give up racing. After all, they had only known each other for a very short time. But even if they had known each other for their whole lives, she couldn't ask that of him.

She realized that Billy just wasn't right for her: she had gotten carried away and had let her imagination get the best of her. Heather's cards had told her she was going to have a mysterious visitor who was going to solve all her problems. Then Billy had appeared. She was angry at herself for being so suggestible.

"I think Mother Nature looks like an Egyptian mummy," Julie said. The five girls on the float committee were in the gym huddled over a mound of papier-mâché that looked worse the more they tried to improve it. They were trying to make a figure of Mother Nature that would be placed in a forest setting. It was pouring rain outside, and all the crepe paper had gotten soaked when they had brought it from the car. The colors had run together into one sad, faded hue, and every time they touched the paper, dye came off on their hands.

"Here's the tape. Let's try to shape her up a bit." Beth tossed the tape to Alison, who wasn't very quick to catch.

She remembered Billy tossing her a wrench. She had missed it by a mile, and he'd ribbed her about it: "So you're not a star out-fielder, huh?"

"Could be—if you gave me a mitt," she had said, laughing.

The memory pinched her face into a frown. She wished she could just forget him—there was no reason to think of Billy now. She figured that they could be friends, but it might be easier if a little time passed first.

It had been over a week since she'd seen him at the track, and she was torn between relief and disappointment that he hadn't tried to contact her.

Alison hung up the damp crepe paper streamers to dry. She had no idea how to hide the water spots, but everyone was so cheerful about the project, it was bound to turn out OK.

Chloe Parker surveyed the mound of papier-mâché that was Mother Nature and clicked her tongue. "I just hope that whoever gets picked as May Queen is prettier than Mother Nature. Heather, maybe if you model for us—" And without waiting for Heather's reply, Chloe started draping strips of crepe paper around Heather's thin frame. The rest of the girls quickly joined in, muffling her giggles by tying crepe paper around her mouth.

"Look! Her neck!" Julie pointed to the torn neckline where Heather was trying to free herself of her wrappings. "She's coming to life!"

Heather staggered toward the others in an imitation of a mummy, while Julie did a mock radio announcement:

"It appears that a mummy from the Egyptian Museum has gotten loose and is prowling about the city. All citizens be on the alert— lock your doors and stay inside. This is a warning—"

She signed off with a muffled scream as Heather's palm clamped over her mouth.

"What happened to that nice Billy Kendall?" Marcy Matlock asked her daughter. "He hasn't been by for a while."

"I asked him not to, Mom," Alison said. Her mother glanced up with a sharp, questioning look, but Alison didn't offer further information.

"I suppose you know best. I just thought he was nice," Mrs. Matlock mumbled.

Alison was helping set the tables for a banquet that Friday evening. Each time the phone rang, and it rang often in the inn, she leaned toward the sound, hoping it was Billy.

But why? Did she just want the opportunity to tell him again that she didn't want to see him?

In any case he hadn't called. Maybe he was afraid she would tell him off. Maybe he was treading lightly for fear of hurting her. Maybe he was giving her time to think about everything, in the hope that she would change her mind. Or, he could have decided that she wasn't worth his time—too sensitive, too hung up on Marty. . . .

Alison toyed with these ideas as she set the tables, taking comfort in the familiar positions of the utensils and the crisp folds of the cloth napkins. A fire blazed in the stone hearth, sending flickering shadows across the beamed ceiling and the white tablecloths. Her father's bent figure, darkly silhouetted in his office, filled her with a sudden warmth. She wanted to hide in his arms, the way she had as a child. She wanted his strong arms to take away all her problems.

Just then, a bicycle touring group began arriving. The group came every year, and Alison always enjoyed their fun and energetic company.

"So how're you doing, Alison?" Mick, the leader of the bike group, asked when the group had all gathered. He dropped a kiss on the end of her nose.

Alison blushed as the other riders chuckled. Mick's girlfriend, Kit, shook her hand warmly.

"Still working on cars?" Kit wanted to know. She did all her own repairs on her bicycle.

"Yup. There's always something to fix." Alison smiled. Mick ruffled her hair playfully and introduced her to some new members of the group.

The cheerful bustle continued as everyone lounged around waiting for dinner. "Hey, let's play some volleyball," Alison suggested, and most of the guests followed her out to the net on the big front lawn.

The evening was warm, and the setting sun still provided enough light so they could see the ball. The highly spirited bicyclists were good players, and Alison was soon concentrating on serves and spikes. It was Mick's turn to serve. Winking at Alison on the other side of the net, he cried, "Get ready for the grand slam, Ally, baby."

And a grand slam it was. The ball came at her so fast that she barely had time to raise her arms. She was all ready for the disappointment of a missed shot when she saw the ball sail back across the net, right back to Mick. There was no one behind her. Who had saved the shot?

She whirled around with the joy of victory on her face, ready to congratulate the quick thinking of her teammates.

"Billy, what are you doing here?" gasped Alison, her expression having instantly changed to one of shock.

"Helping you win your volleyball game," he said lightly. "Hey, keep your eye on the ball."

With a thud the ball fell at her feet.

"Looks like you need me on your team," said Billy.

Alison looked around in embarrassment. She thought she should leave the game and not even speak to Billy, but the group of eager players was hard to resist, and the ball was already being handed to Billy for the next serve.

Alison didn't have to face Billy one-on-one until the dinner bell sounded and the guests sprinted toward the dining room. Billy and Alison lingered on the lawn.

"I brought you something," Billy said, and they walked over to his truck. He leaned in the window, and Alison's eyes fell fondly on his strong back. He handed her a wooden gear-shift knob.

"Oh, thanks, Billy. It's just what I wanted."

He laughed. "Do you realize how crazy that sounds? Most girls would rather have a diamond."

"I'm not most girls," Alison reminded him.

He studied her for a moment. "I know. I think that's why I came over tonight."

She blushed, not knowing what to say. His words stunned her. Suddenly she wanted to throw herself into his arms. But she just stood in silence, not knowing how to deal with all her conflicting emotions.

Billy broke the silence by reaching back into his car. This time he handed her a bouquet of tiny lavender roses. "Just so you don't think I forgot the other part of you."

"Oh, they're beautiful, Billy. Thank you. They're my favorite color. How'd you know?"

"Lavender just seems to suit you."

Another awkward moment of silence followed. Alison kept the bouquet of roses over her mouth, pretending to smell them but mostly trying to hide her trembling lips.

Finally Billy said, "I don't know how to say this to you, Alison. So, I guess I'll just say it." For a moment he stared across the wide lawn at the setting sun. Then he turned to face her. "I understand how you must feel about me, but I want you to know I don't want to lose your friendship."

Alison frowned. Friendship? Did Billy think of her just as a friend? If that was the case, what difference did all this make to her? She felt confused, light-headed. Ever since the race she'd been on edge, and now seeing him and hearing his words made her even more tense. "Thank you," she told him stiffly.

"I wouldn't want to hurt you, Alison," he continued. "But I have this crazy idea that maybe, through me, you can overcome your fears."

Fears. The word shot through Alison's head. Yes, she was afraid, and not only of racing. She was afraid of opening herself to love.

"Aren't you expecting a lot, Billy?" she questioned him. "Don't forget who you're talking to. I didn't have any fears until Marty's accident. I thought racing was all fun. I thought nothing bad could possibly happen."

"Marty was unlucky. You know the statistics," Billy said matter-of-factly.

"Marty became a statistic," she said, thinking, *What do I do if you're unlucky, Billy? What do I do if I lose you to a race?*

"I'm not heartless." Billy tapped his chest with two fingers. "Just because I don't agree with you—"

"I know that."

"I'm racing Sunday. Do you want to go? I can get you a ticket."

Alison shook her head, the hurt building to a bursting level. His presence upset her. "I don't think I can, Billy. I don't think I can watch you race at all."

He shrugged. "OK, just no hard feelings, huh? I do other things besides race, you know—just so you don't think I'm an accident looking for a place to happen."

Alison smiled.

"Do you want to go out tonight?"

Billy's brilliant grin and the laughter in his blue eyes loosened something inside Alison. She laughed. "OK, let's go out. We'd have to make it later, though. I have to help serve dinner."

"That's OK. I have to work tonight till nine, anyway. I asked for an hour off so that I could come over here, and I've got to get back. Would you mind meeting me at Whoppin' Donuts?"

"No, I wouldn't mind. I'll see you at nine." Even as she spoke the words, she wondered what had made her agree to go out with him again. How could she do it to herself? She knew she couldn't see him without growing closer to him, and getting close to him meant danger.

He pulled her to him before turning to leave, brushing his lips against her hair and stroking her cheek fondly.

"Don't be afraid, Alison. I mean it. Everything's going to be OK," he said softly, and then he let her go before she could reply.

There was something irresistible about

him. With a twinge of fear, she suspected it might be the same "something" that had bound her to Marty—that unquenchable spirit.

Chapter Eight

At every stoplight Alison considered turning the car around and going back home. But she found herself pulling into the parking lot of Whoppin' Donuts, almost numb to the fact that she was going out with Billy. Hadn't she decided not to see him again? Her parents had always joked that they should have named her Rhino because she was so tough, but now she felt like a jellyfish. Nothing seemed more important than being with Billy.

Alison still wondered if he just wanted to be friends with her. As she caught a glimpse of him through the plate glass window of the doughnut shop, she knew that her pounding heart was definitely more than a friendly reaction. If he just wanted to be her friend, she would have to cool herself down a lot.

As she pushed open the heavy door, she was greeted by Billy's grin.

"Hi, Alison. Can you wait a couple of minutes while we finish cleaning up?"

"Sure." Alison perched on a bar stool and watched the clean-up process. Soon Billy was through and had changed into Levis and a striped T-shirt.

Suddenly something flew through the air and hit Billy smack on the head.

"Oh, no, you guys—not the doughnut holes!" Billy groaned. But he couldn't resist returning the shot. He grabbed a handful of doughnut holes and threw them at the guy nearest him.

"You'll never finish the clean-up," cried Alison, but she had barely completed her sentence when two doughnut holes landed on her lap.

"Catch," said a boy, who started juggling three doughnut holes over the freshly wiped counter. Crumbs were spilling everywhere, and the air was filled with laughter and whooping war cries.

"I'm leaving before this place is totally wrecked," announced Billy, charging for the door.

"Oh, yeah?"

"Hey, I'm going on a date. Try and keep me here one minute longer." Billy caught the three doughnut holes that came spinning toward him. Then he grabbed Alison's hand, and they escaped under heavy doughnut fire.

Outside, Alison burst into laughter. "What a bunch of crazies!"

"I thought they'd gag us with doughnut holes before we got out of there." Billy shook his head.

Alison dusted off her blouse. "Now I'm covered with sugar."

Billy grinned and kissed the sugary tip of her nose. "Makes you even sweeter than you already are. Easier to get stuck to."

Alison groaned but couldn't help laughing. She wiped the sugar granules off his cheek. "You're pretty sweet, yourself."

They drove in Alison's car to the movie theater, where they saw an Eddie Murphy movie. Alison laughed so hard her stomach ached.

"Let's get something to eat," Billy suggested as they were leaving the theater.

"If my poor stomach can handle it."

"All those jokes can be dangerous to your health."

Billy laced his fingers through hers. The movie had put them both in good moods.

"Eddie Murphy sure does great impersonations. He's like a split personality," commented Billy.

"Well, he sure split my sides," replied Alison.

"Hey! Let's get banana splits. It'll fit in with the rest of our evening."

They lingered at the ice-cream parlor, recalling some of the funnier scenes of the movie. As they drove back to Whoppin' Donuts, where Billy's truck was parked, Alison was glad the conversation hadn't turned to racing. If they didn't talk about it, she could pretend it didn't exist.

Of course, she knew it was foolish to think that way. She wanted to enjoy Billy—not a hard thing to do—without any gnawing fears. If only things were different. . . .

Alison stopped her car in the parking lot. He turned to her. For the first time that evening, his face was serious. He traced her lips with his finger and casually moved it along her cheekbone to stroke her long hair.

He cleared his throat, and Alison knew he was going to say something important. Perhaps he would tell her he didn't think they should see each other again—there were too many conflicts. That night they had avoided any topics that could bring these conflicts to the surface. But Alison knew they existed, and she knew Billy knew. She couldn't help but worry.

"I think I love you, Alison."

Her heart stopped. She wasn't ready to hear that. She had been expecting to hear "Let's be friends" or "Sorry, it just won't work." It was too unbelievable that he would love her.

"You do?" she responded, licking her lips to soothe the sudden dryness in her mouth.

"Does that surprise you?" He wrapped a length of her silken hair around his little finger. "How do you feel about me?"

His eyes searched hers, and her flesh quivered under his stare. How did she feel, besides scared? "I think I do—too."

He read her thoughts. "Are you afraid to say 'love'?" he questioned.

Alison was silent for a moment. "I'm just plain afraid."

"I know. But maybe after a time, it won't be so scary." He kissed her forehead, and they sat in silence for a long time. Alison was afraid to look at Billy but kept his hand in hers, playing with his long, slender fingers and staring out into the darkness.

Billy broke the silence. "Hey, Al, the

antique car show opens tomorrow. I have to work in the morning but I thought I'd go in the afternoon. Do you want to come?"

She wondered if she should go. Hadn't she told herself to cool it? But that was when she thought he just wanted to be her friend. Now she knew he loved her. But that didn't help her; she still felt confused and torn. Part of her knew that she could be hurt badly, just the way she had been hurt by Marty. She should protect herself from a similar experience. But her heart yearned for the warmth and fun of Billy. She wanted to let herself fall head over heels.

"How about it, Alison? Is it a date?" Billy's brown eyes met her own, prompting her.

"Yes, it's a date. I'd like to go."

"Good. I'll pick you up around one."

"I see Billy's around again," Alison's father said the next morning at breakfast. "How's his racing going?"

"Racing?" snapped Alison. "Why ask about his racing? There's more to Billy than racing, you know. He likes to design parts and work on engines, too. I don't think he's a fanatic, or anything."

"I'm sorry," replied her father, giving

Alison a knowing look. "I just asked a simple question. You don't have to jump down my throat."

Then he squeezed her shoulder gently. "I don't want you getting hurt, honey. You're not as tough as you sometimes seem. I suppose you're too old now to be protected, but when you told us that Billy races—"

"Mr. Matlock, excuse me." It was Ellie, the chambermaid. "There are some guests here asking for rooms."

"I'll see you later, Dad," Alison told him as he hurried off.

"Have a good time," he called over his shoulder.

Her father's words swirled in her head. She knew he meant well, but she did not need to hear his worries. They were too much like her own, and she didn't want to face the issue of racing just yet.

"Are you free as a bird this afternoon?" Billy asked Alison when he arrived.

She climbed onto the seat next to him. "Not quite. I have to be back to help with dinner. We have twenty people coming tonight."

"Don't worry—we'll be home on time."

As they drove along the highway, Alison's

tensions disappeared. The day was beautiful, the sun poured through the young blossoms on the trees, crops were springing up in the brown fields, and a scent of new-mown hay was in the air.

And Billy was beside her—that was the best part. She really did love him. She and Billy together were something special—what was she worrying about?

Billy knew a lot about old cars. He could guess the model and the year of practically every car at the show.

"One of these days I'd like to collect old cars and bikes." He was looking at a white '57 Chevy.

"What a beaut," he said and whistled. "You can almost see the saddle shoes and hear the doo-wap of Elvis." He started snapping his fingers to an imaginary song.

"You know the words to those old songs?" she asked teasingly.

"Yeah, don't tell anybody, but I'm really kind of old-fashioned. I still believe in Chevys, rock 'n' roll, and love." He kissed her on the lips, right in front of the judge's stand. Two boys leaning against a Model T whistled.

Alison blushed, but she couldn't help giggling at their reactions.

Billy sang fifties songs all the way home. Alison hummed along with him, listening to the words. All the songs were about love.

"If someone landed here from outer space, they'd think we earthlings had one-track minds," observed Alison.

"We do," Billy said. "We want what's hardest to find."

She studied the curve of Billy's neck. Then her gaze traveled to where his eyebrows met his thick curls.

Without thinking, she reached over and squeezed the back of his neck. He smiled at her, his lips slightly parted.

Alison thought about what Billy had said—"We want what's hardest to find." Well, she had wanted to find somebody to help her get over Marty. Now it looked like she had someone. But would he help her get over Marty? Or would he repeat that old nightmare for her, making the pain even worse? If she could put in an order for the perfect boyfriend, he would be a Billy without the racing.

Maybe love wasn't made to order, she considered. But as Billy's hand moved toward hers, she wondered what she was complaining about. If she wanted it, she had, at her fingertips, what was hardest to find.

Chapter Nine

In the dream Alison was weightless. She floated a few inches above the bleachers at the track. She wanted to clutch the metal railing, but her fingers couldn't reach it, and all she could feel was the wind sifting through them.

Marty was in the lineup, tucked into his car away from her view. The sun reflected off the car's silver finish, blinding her. The crowd's roar was like a living force that, combined with the heavy air, choked Alison. Suddenly a feeling of horror sent her earthward, groping for her seat and gasping for air.

The starting gun sounded. Marty's car shot from the lineup as though from a cannon, and dust billowed around him. Alison thrilled at the sight, and the deafening roar made her skin rise in goose bumps.

She raised her binoculars to see Marty go around the first curve. Cars screeched around it, and one turned over and over. The driver emerged, unhurt. Alison could see he'd taken the turn wrong. At least Marty knew how to take turns, he never made mistakes. . . .

There was a sudden shriek of tires. A car was out of control, hitting the guardrail, flipping onto its roof. Another car charged into it, spinning it like a top. The crowd's screams mingled with her own. "Marty, Marty, Marty," echoed in her head.

Then the suffocating odor of smoke filled her lungs. Alison wished with all her might that it wasn't Marty under the rubble.

She ran while medics dragged Marty's body from the wreckage. She couldn't get to him; her legs would only carry her—it was as if she were running in slow motion. A blast of foam hit the flaming car, extinguishing the blaze and her view. She was running, crying, trying to reach him, her feet were as heavy as lead. She felt as if she were running through water. . . .

Alison awoke to the sound of the phone ringing.

"Al, are you coming with us today?" It was Julie.

"Where to?" Alison blinked sleep from her eyes, the image of Marty's accident still fresh in her mind. She couldn't remember making any definite plans.

"It's Sunday. The race—Billy's race. Aren't you going?" she questioned. "We're watching Steve again."

The news was like a splash of cold water. Billy had mentioned his Sunday race, but she had wanted to change the subject and had completely put it out of her mind.

"Didn't you and Billy talk about it? I mean, you two spent the entire weekend together practically, since Friday night. I thought you'd get free passes."

"He told me Friday evening, Julie, but I forgot. I guess I didn't really want to know about it."

"Oh, Al." Julie heaved a sigh. "I'm sorry."

"Well, don't be." Alison felt awful. She had awakened to another nightmare.

"You're getting along with him OK, aren't you?" Julie asked.

"Yeah. Too well, if you ask me. Maybe it would be easier if we didn't get along."

"Don't be silly, Al. He's just your type. Cheer up about him, will you? Listen, Heather and I are coming over. When we get there, you can decide whether or not you want to go."

Alison hauled herself out of bed and

stared in the mirror before taking a shower. *If you're going to love Billy*, she told her reflection, *you're going to have to separate yourself from his racing. It's not going to be easy, but it's the only way.*

When Heather and Julie came over, Alison fixed coffee and bagels. They sat out on the porch and talked about the weekend.

"Billy and I discussed his racing, and I said I didn't think I could watch him again," Alison said.

"Are you just going to ignore the fact that he races?" Heather asked.

"I don't know whether that's possible," Julie added.

"Well, he does understand how I feel, Julie. I just have to keep my cool about the whole thing." Alison ran her finger along the rim of her coffee cup. "We had such a good time this weekend." She told them about the car show on Saturday and the movie Friday night.

"We told you so. You *are* in love!"

"Come on, you guys," Alison protested and smiled in spite of herself. She didn't mention the fact that Billy had said he loved her. That was a little nugget of gold that she wanted to keep secret.

"If you aren't in love," Julie insisted, "then you've got the worst case of blushes I've ever seen."

"Isn't anyone going to ask me about my weekend?" Heather demanded.

"How was it with Barry?" Alison gladly turned the focus of conversation to her friend.

"Just wonderful. The only thing that bothers me is that he still doesn't kiss very well."

"Give him time," Alison said.

"True love overlooks all flaws," Julie said.

"Just think if he complained about your bony elbows, Heather," Alison said, knowing how Heather felt about her elbows.

"Oh, let's not talk about my elbows!" She moaned. "Do you really think they're ugly, Al? Really?"

Julie and Alison cracked up.

"You guys are mean," Heather decided. "By the way, tomorrow after school we'll consult the cards again. I want to find out about Barry."

"Yeah, and while you're at it, I want to know something. I thought the cards said my mysterious visitor would solve all my problems," challenged Alison. "It seems like Billy has *caused* all my problems."

"Well, are you going to wait for an answer from the cards before you make up your mind about the race today?" Julie brought them back to reality. "Come on, we're going to be late. You coming, Al?"

Alison drew a deep breath and shook her head. "No. Maybe someday I can watch, but not yet."

"Is this the same thick-skinned person we used to know?" Heather quipped.

"I'm sorry to be such a party pooper," replied Alison, and then she tried to lighten things up a bit. "But keep an eye on Billy for me. I don't want him smiling at too many cute girls." She strolled outside with them to examine a new dent in the side of Julie's car. "I don't know, Jules. It's pretty bad, but I can try banging it out with a hammer. Drop it off when you get back from the race."

"See you later, Al." Heather tucked her long legs into the passenger seat.

"Yeah. Let me know who wins," she called out. A lump formed in her throat as she waved goodbye.

It was impossible for Alison not to think of Billy. She prepared breakfast for a few guests who were late risers and then went outside.

She needed to keep busy, and her father had told her there were some flats of pansies that needed to be planted. She picked up a spade and began the task of putting the flowers in the ground.

Strains of a Mozart piano concerto drifted out from her father's office. Alison loved her father's music. They favored the same measured, ordered pieces. Somehow the music helped her organize her chaotic feelings and made her feel calmer and more in control.

But really, everything flowed perfectly with Billy. Julie and Heather would be surprised if they knew just how well she got along with Billy. He was so understanding—not like the other boys she had briefly dated. They had all seemed afraid of her. Either they were afraid because she knew more about cars than they did, or they were afraid to touch her in case the memory of Marty should come surging out like a bursting dam. Billy understood the pain that Alison felt, but he didn't treat her like a china doll. He treated her like an adult who knew how to take care of herself.

There was one thing that she was quite sure Billy did not know. And that was how frequently she thought of him. Marty's face was becoming a blur to her, and in its place was Billy's image.

Is it OK to be so adaptable? Alison asked herself, feeling slightly guilty.

Her mother rode the lawnmower over to where Alison was working and switched off the engine.

"How's it going?" she asked, shading her eyes from the midday sun with her hand.

"Fine."

"Where's Billy today?"

"Racing." Alison pronounced the word without emotion.

"And you're not watching?" Her mother's eyebrows arched in surprise.

"No."

"I can understand why you don't want to watch, Allie," Mrs. Matlock said sympathetically. "I just wonder how it's going to work out between the two of you."

"We get along fine."

"So I noticed. And your father and I also noticed that you are living again. That's nice to see." She hesitated for a moment, examining her fingernails. "Sometimes it can be painful, but there's a certain amount of risk taking in life."

"So I'm finding out."

Marcy Matlock smiled, her slender, tanned arms reaching for the steering wheel. "I'm here if you need me."

"Thanks," Alison said as her mother drove away. And she meant it.

Alison finished smoothing earth around the young plants, then carried the empty plastic containers up to the garden shed and went inside to wash the grit from her hands.

The phone rang as Alison entered the kitchen.

"Alison." It was Heather. She spoke her name with finality, but her voice was small, unsure.

"Yes. What is it, Heather?"

There was a pause as Heather took a deep breath. "Billy's hurt. They don't know how bad it is, but he's going to the hospital now."

Alison closed her eyes and tried to breathe to clear the sudden dizziness that swamped her head.

"Al, are you still there?"

Barely, she thought. She nodded, then realized that Heather couldn't see her. "Yes. Is he—?" She couldn't bring herself to ask too many questions. She wanted to know everything, but she also didn't want to know anything. The dream of the night before hung in front of her eyes, and she blinked to clear it.

"He's unconscious, Al."

Unconscious, that means he's not dead. It also means that he's badly hurt. Alison swallowed hard, but her throat was dry. Her tongue stuck to the roof of her mouth. "I'm going to the hospital," she managed to say.

"Want me to pick you up?"

"No, I'll go right now from here. Which hospital?" The rushing in her ears made Heather's reply almost inaudible.

"Brentwood."

When Alison got off the phone, her father was standing next to her, waiting.

"Billy's hurt," Alison announced, although she needn't have bothered. He knew from her expression. Perhaps she already knew, too. Perhaps the dream was an omen. The driver in her dream had been Marty, but it could just as easily have been Billy. She should have stopped him. She could have tried.

Her mother appeared in the doorway. She had seen her daughter like this before and instantly knew something was wrong.

"I'm going to the hospital," Alison announced stiffly.

"We'll drive you, Al. You're in no shape to drive." Her father's quiet insistence offered some comfort. Like a little child, Alison took his hand, while her mother went off to gather car keys and pocketbook.

The sterile odor of the hospital filled Alison's senses, making her stomach churn. She hated that smell, and she hated the memories that came with it: the smell of burning rubber, the crackle of flames, the image of Marty, lifeless.

The ride to the hospital had felt so strangely familiar. At one point she had wanted the car to stop so that she could get out. She wanted to go back to the garden, hide, forget. But she couldn't change a thing. She felt so helpless, sitting in the car while the world whizzed by. Her legs were heavy and still, like in the dream. She remembered whispering in Marty's ear, the words tumbling out of her mouth as if in a rush to get said before . . .

Her arms felt empty—the same feeling she had had after Marty died. As she walked into the waiting room and saw Billy's parents there, she thought of Marty's sobbing mother.

Trembling, Alison sat down next to Billy's

mother. Mrs. Kendall explained what had happened.

"Billy crashed into a tree after another kid swerved into him. He's broken his ankle, and he's damaged a kidney. They're operating on it right now."

Mrs. Kendall's fingers, lightly covering Alison's, were ice-cold. She wore a floral print skirt, and her hair was pulled back into a bun.

"Were you at the race?" Billy's father asked. He wore faded blue jeans and tortoise-shell framed glasses perched on his nose.

"Uh, no, I wasn't," Alison said quickly. She didn't want to explain herself to Billy's parents. They probably didn't know about Marty, and it wouldn't make them feel any better to know that she had been through this before, and that the last time her boyfriend had died.

She closed her eyes, a rush of images filling the darkness—Billy's crazy grin, his freckled nose, the way he wore a cap pulled down over his brow . . .

Her father brought her a cup of coffee. He had to hold it for her while she sipped because her hands trembled so.

Alison recalled Billy saying that people wanted what was hardest to find. *When we*

101

finally find it, is it always taken away? she wondered. *When I find somebody to love, is he always going to disappear?*

Two hours passed. The waiting seemed like an eternity, but finally Billy's doctor emerged from the operating room.

"The operation was a success," he told Billy's parents. "We've oversewn the laceration, and Billy is resting comfortably now."

"Will he be all right?" Mrs. Kendall asked. Her voice quivered.

Alison was thinking of Marty and how serious the doctor had looked when asked that same question.

"It will take him a while to recuperate, but he should be fine," the doctor said. "You can see him now."

"Come on," Mr. Kendall whispered in Alison's ear. "You can come, too."

The nurse frowned at him, but he tugged at Alison's elbow. Dutifully, she followed him.

Billy was still asleep. He lay in a sea of white, hooked up to IVs, his usually vibrant, sun-browned face now a pale, sickly color. His hair was rumpled with sweat against the pillow. His hand lay upturned on the top of the sheet. Alison thought he looked like a little boy.

She loved him. And, she realized, as tears leaked out the corners of her eyes, that she didn't want to.

Chapter Ten

Alison moved like a sleepwalker through the next hours. She went home and tried to rest, but she waited anxiously for news about Billy. Heather came over and insisted on going with Alison to the hospital that evening, saying she'd wait outside in the corridor.

Alison quietly entered Billy's room. He was still groggy and could only manage a weak "hi."

She did all the talking. It reminded her so much of when Marty had been lying in a coma. At least Billy was conscious.

She tried to seem cheerful and confident. She talked about the float the committee was building.

"We've got this huge blob of papier-mâché that's supposed to look like Mother Nature, but it just looks like blobs of papier-mâché. We're going to take it to an art class to see what can be done with it. Otherwise, it's not

104

going to be featured in the parade. I mean, who wants a blobby Mother Nature?"

Billy's mouth turned up slightly in a smile. He looked awfully weak. The nurse came in and told Alison she had three or four more minutes, and then she would have to leave.

"Then we have a flowered canopy where the queen will sit. I hope you'll be better by then, so you can see it," she said, smoothing damp curls off his forehead.

He smiled again and squeezed her hand.

"It's time to go, Alison. Billy has to rest now," the nurse told her.

Alison stopped her nervous chatter. Gently she said, "See you tomorrow, Billy." Alison leaned over and kissed his forehead, which felt cool.

"How'd it go?" Heather asked when Alison came out into the corridor.

"He's weak, but he can smile and talk a little. The nurse says he'll be much better tomorrow, after the painkillers wear off a bit. It's just a relief to see his eyes open."

Heather squeezed her hand. "He'll be fine, Al, don't worry. You know, I talked to him before the race. He said he wished you had come."

"I bet he doesn't wish that now." She sighed.

"Are you up for getting something to eat? It might be good for you," Heather said.

"I'm not really hungry, but I'll go with you. "You eat, I'll watch."

At the restaurant Alison sipped on a Coke and tried to keep up a conversation with Heather, but her mind never strayed far from Billy.

The next afternoon after school she drove to the hospital. Billy had been moved to another more cheerful room, next to a window. Flowers filled the nightstand.

Billy looked better. There was a little color in his cheeks, and he smiled more readily when she entered the room.

"How're you feeling?" she asked, leaning over to kiss him.

"Better, but not exactly normal." He grinned at her. His voice was still weak, missing its familiar ring of laughter.

"I'm so relieved you're going to be OK," Alison said, sitting down at his side, her heart beating fast.

"I know." He moved his fingers along the sheet to grasp hers. "I'm glad you're here."

"I love you, Billy." Those words came out

so easily now. Yet she ached inside. She didn't feel she could ever go through this pain again. When he was well, she planned to tell him she couldn't go on loving him. She couldn't bear to see him hurt. If there had been any doubt before, there was none now—she knew she couldn't love a racer.

Not attending his races wouldn't solve the problem. He could get hurt whether or not she was there. She couldn't go on ignoring Billy's racing; it was part of him, important to him. Alison knew that she was up against something that would eventually come between their love for each other.

Billy's hand closed around hers and squeezed tightly. His grip was still strong and made her tingle. "Alison, I've been doing some thinking."

Alison held her breath. Was he going to tell her not to love him anymore? Was he going to tell her to forget about him?

"The doctors told me this morning that I damaged a kidney. It's fixed now, but if I bounce it around much more, I could permanently damage it. I can't afford that. Breaking an ankle is one thing, but I can't abuse myself to the point of no repair." He paused and cleared his throat. "I'm quitting motocross, Alison."

Alison blinked hard, not sure if she'd heard him right. "Are you sure?"

"I'm positive. I have to. And it's not as if I don't have other things to do. Safe things. I can keep my foot in the door building and designing bikes. I love doing those things, and I can always watch the races from the bleachers." He grinned.

Alison wanted to melt with relief. "Billy, I hate to see your body banged up like this. And if it's really as serious as you say—"

"It is. I can still ride, but I can't smash myself up like this by racing. It made you awfully nervous, anyway, so maybe it's for the best."

"That's strictly my problem, Billy."

"Yeah, but I can't stop you from feeling how you do, and I think eventually it would've divided us. I love you, Alison. And there shouldn't be anything pulling us apart."

She kissed him tenderly, shivering at his words. She felt totally unafraid right then. It seemed that nothing could take Billy away from her now.

"Guess what! I've been nominated for May Day queen!" Heather announced ecstatically the next day.

The three girls were sitting in the quad, eating lunch. Julie grimaced at her yogurt and carrot sticks, enviously eying slim Heather as she pulled the wrapper off a candy bar.

"There are ten others nominated, so I may not make the finals. They choose only four princesses and one queen from the bunch," Heather went on. "But it's still an honor."

"We have a celebrity in our midst, Al. Can you believe it?" Julie nibbled daintily on a carrot.

"Congratulations, Heather. I knew those bony elbows were OK!" Alison gave her friend a huge hug.

"You look better today, Alison," Julie noted, "now that you know Billy's going to be OK."

Alison had gone back to the hospital the evening before, then had had to do a lot of homework, so, other than telling her friends that Billy would be all right, she hadn't had time to tell them what had happened. "I am. But Billy had a close call. The doctors don't think he should race anymore. He says he's quitting."

"Seriously?"

"He suffered some kidney damage," she

explained. "But they say he'll be fine as long as he doesn't race."

"Does this solve all your problems, or what?" Heather stated. "The cards were right after all," she joked.

Alison felt drained. Yes, it did seem as if her troubles were over. But it made her feel a little sick that a serious accident had to happen to make her dreams come true.

"I guess my problems are solved," she said aloud. "Except that I never wanted Billy to get hurt. I was just beginning to try to work things out for myself."

"Hey, I've got an idea." Julie threw her empty yogurt container into the trash bin. "Let's have a get-well party for Billy after he gets home from the hospital. How long will he be in there?"

"I think about a week."

"Perfect. We'll plan it for the weekend after. Talk to his mom and see what she says, and then it's full speed ahead!"

The party was held at the inn. Alison's closest friends as well as many of Billy's were there.

Julie had insisted on being in charge of the food. She had prepared a beautiful buffet of cheeses, cold cuts, vegetables with dips, and homemade breads. She had even baked a huge chocolate cake.

Billy sat on a chair, his crutches beside him, and a group stood around him, waiting to sign his cast.

"You sure you don't want me to sign autographs?" Billy joked, waving his pen in the air.

"Who wants your autograph, Kendall?" his friend Joe called out. "You lost your last race!"

"He's a hero 'cause he came out of it in one piece," someone else said.

"Almost one piece." Billy grinned.

Alison caught his eye, and he winked at her. She was across the room, serving lemonade.

"Hey, didn't you used to be Marty Willins's girlfriend?" a tall boy with the beginnings of a mustache asked her.

"Yes."

"I heard about him. Sorry," he said sincerely.

"It's OK. It was a year ago."

"How do you know Billy?" he wanted to know.

111

"We met at the junkyard," she told him. "I work on cars."

His eyes lit up. "No kidding?"

Some of the couples started dancing. Billy hobbled over to Alison's side.

"I'd dance with you, Alison, but I'm feeling clumsy tonight," he teased.

"Uh, thanks anyway, Billy. If you stepped on my toes, I might need a cast, too."

"Sounds romantic," replied Billy. "We could play great footsies together."

Julie and Heather breezed by to say hello.

"Congratulations, Heather," Billy said. "I hear you might be joining beautiful Mother Nature on the float."

Heather pointed to Billy's cast. "Save my autograph! It might be a collector's item someday."

"How's the float coming?"

"We think it's afloat," Julie said, and everyone groaned.

"Billy, when's your next race?" his friend Joe asked.

Alison dropped her smile. She'd known someone was going to ask this question and had been dreading the moment.

"Never, Joe. I'm giving up racing," Billy replied, his voice firm and steady.

"Is that right? This is a goodbye party then?"

"No, I'll still be around."

"Sounds like you're afraid," Joe baited him.

"I'm afraid, yeah. With good reason."

Alison detected the annoyance in Billy's voice. She wished Joe would stop testing him.

"Billy, you're so good. Why do you want to quit?" someone else joined in.

"Doctor's orders, Sam. My kidney was damaged."

"Really?" Sam clicked his tongue. "Man, nothing short of World War Three could keep me off the track. I thought you were pretty crazy about motocross, too."

"Sure, I'm crazy about motocross, but I'm not crazy. I'd have to be to keep racing after what happened to me."

"Yeah?" Joe and Sam didn't look convinced.

"That's right," Billy said. "I'll keep up with things by fixing and building bikes. Maybe I'll even design some parts."

"You always were good at that," Joe offered.

"And I can get better at it, too." Billy's grin warmed Alison. "Maybe Al and I will even go into business together." He slid his arm around her waist, and the other boys wandered away.

"I'm glad we're together," he said, squeezing her hard. "I think we're good for each other."

"Me, too." She was so relieved to hear Billy stick up for his decision.

"They don't understand," Billy said, "because they've never been badly hurt. I didn't really understand either, until it happened to me."

You don't know how glad that makes me, Alison said to herself. Now, she didn't have to be afraid of losing him. She was suddenly free—free enough to love him.

Chapter Eleven

"I think this float's just about ready to roll," Julie said as she and two other girls twisted crepe paper around the base of the truck bed. "Isn't it beautiful?"

"Yeah. I just hope it looks this good once it's out in daylight," Beth said. "We might notice all the flaws."

With the help of the art class, Mother Nature had been vastly improved. She actually looked human, and the wide crepe paper drapings gave her dress a fairylike look that everyone thought was suitable. She was placed opposite the arch where the May Day queen would sit.

"Tomorrow's the big day, isn't it, Heather? But now that Mother Nature looks so good, you have really stiff competition for the queen."

"I'm not going to sleep a wink. I'll probably have huge bags under my eyes tomorrow."

"Hey, it's early," Chloe noticed. "We didn't plan to be finished so soon. Want to celebrate with ice cream?"

"I'm meeting Billy at the track. He's watching a friend try out a new part on his bike," Alison said. "I'm heading over there now." Then she added, "Good luck, Heather. I'll be thinking of you."

"Won't we all!" cried Julie.

Alison left the barn where the float was being assembled, glad that it was finished. The past week had been hectic. She hadn't seen much of Billy.

She pulled onto the grounds surrounding the practice track. In the distance bikes roared over hills, their riders looking like tiny black insects on a leafy background. One of them lagged far behind, obviously not part of the practice competition.

Alison stood behind two boys who leaned against the metal railing. They talked loudly over the roar of engines.

"Since the accident, he's been scared. Says he's not racing again," said one.

"Billy? Not race? You're joking!" The other boy was shorter, with black curly hair and a bandaged elbow.

"No, it's true. Doctor's orders, he says.

116

But a lot of people think it just scared him to death. His girlfriend used to go out with Marty Willins, the stock-car racer."

"Oh, yeah. Bet she's scared, too—probably threw a temper tantrum until he promised to quit."

It took all of Alison's self-control to keep from butting in to the conversation. She didn't want people thinking she was responsible for Billy's quitting! But, she supposed, it was only natural that they would think that after what had happened to Marty. Still, it made her furious.

"Look, there he is!" The taller boy pointed to the track.

Alison moved away from them so that she could watch and wait for Billy in peace. She glanced in the direction the boy pointed.

The boys' attention was fixed on the slow rider. He chugged along, driving around the jumps instead of taking them.

Alison saw the below-the-knee cast. It was definitely Billy. *Why is he out here? He was supposed to be watching a friend try out a new part.*

As if in reply to her question, the other boy said, "He must be racing this weekend.

Guess he's not listening to the doctor after all."

So, Billy couldn't resist. He was practicing for a race. *If I hadn't arrived early,* Alison thought, *I would never have found out. He could race and deceive me for a little longer.*

I should never have believed that he would quit. Alison's anger and disappointment were building. *He likes racing too much to give it up. It doesn't matter what the doctor's orders were. It doesn't matter what I want.*

The track blurred in front of her. Alison wiped at her sudden hot tears as she ran back to her car. She certainly couldn't face Billy now.

It rained that night, and the inn was quiet. All the guests were in their rooms. Alison went to get wood for a fire. As she was putting the first log in place, her mother called, "Billy's on the phone!"

Alison started at the mention of his name. She picked up the downstairs phone.

"Why didn't you come down to the track? I waited hours for you, Alison. Did something come up?" he asked.

"I was there, Billy."

"Where? Are you invisible? I looked all over." He chuckled.

"No, I was there. I saw you on the track, and I left." She pronounced this with finality. "I saw you riding, and some boys standing in front of me said you were practicing for a race. I guess you decided to disobey the doctor."

"I wasn't practicing!" he cried.

Alison felt very far away from him. "Billy," she said coldly, "I don't want you to have to make excuses or tell me some story just to save me the pain."

"Alison, you're not listening to me! Do you really think I'm going to race with a broken ankle and a screwed-up kidney, for crying out loud?" His voice had risen an octave. She moved the receiver away from her ear.

"I don't know, Billy. I don't ever know what you're going to do next. That's up to you. I just know I can't handle this whole thing. I thought your health would be enough of a reason to quit racing, but now it looks like it isn't. Goodbye, Billy."

Alison hung up before she could hear further protests and before she burst into tears. Feeling small, cold, and alone, she wrapped herself in an afghan and sat in front of the fire.

119

Chapter Twelve

"Congratulations, Queenie," Alison told Heather, giving her a kiss on her flushed cheek.

Heather was wearing the flowered crown of the May Day queen and a long, pale blue dress that made her thin figure look full and feminine. Her voice bubbled with joy. "Did you bring your flowers and costume, Al?"

"Got the flowers, got the costume." Alison produced a wicker basket full of paper flowers, which she was to throw from Heather's float. Her costume was a pink jumpsuit, and she had braided pink and yellow ribbons in her hair.

The restroom where they were changing was a madhouse. All of the princesses were busy with last-minute details. They wore long pastel dresses. Every sink was littered with makeup and brushes and combs. Stray ribbons and flowers littered the counters.

One girl tried frantically to repair a snag in her stocking, and two other girls were fixing a shoe strap with a safety pin. The teacher in charge of the parade kept everyone jumping by calling out the time. "Five more minutes, girls. Now hurry."

"You think anyone will notice my shoe?" Delia asked.

"We can always bury it in crepe paper," Beth said, trying to calm her.

"Three more minutes!" screamed the teacher.

The excitement was growing, and Alison and Julie gathered around Heather. "You look fantastic, kid," said Julie. "I think I'll go on a starvation diet tomorrow. You're quite an inspiration."

"Even Mother Nature came out looking OK," said Alison, getting caught up in the bubbling energy. "Now if only my ribbons didn't look like seaweed in a monster's hair," she said. But despite her jokes she kept thinking about how rude she had been to Billy the night before.

After she had hung up on him, Alison worried about what she had done. Maybe she should have given him more of a chance to explain himself, instead of jumping to conclusions. But she couldn't hide her disappointment and anger. The old chaos of her feelings had just swamped her. She had felt out of control again.

If Billy chose to go ahead and disobey his doctor, then what could Alison do? She couldn't dictate to him. She would just have to forget Billy—it obviously wasn't working out.

The float looked beautiful. A flowered arbor made up of every spring blossom imaginable formed an arch behind Heather, who stood on a small raised platform. Her princesses stood around her, holding small bouquets.

Alison stood on the far end of the float and tossed flowers to the crowd as the parade moved slowly through the street. It was hard to smile so much, but the perfect weather and the enthusiastic crowd lifted her spirits.

Alison saw her parents standing next to Heather's. Her father whistled loudly, and her mother waved. Alison threw them extra flowers, which they tried to catch over the bobbing heads in front of them.

Suddenly she saw Billy. Alison was surprised to see him catch a flower and place it between his teeth, like a performer in a nightclub. He looked so funny—leaning on crutches with a paper peony in his mouth. She had to laugh.

"Is that Billy?" Chloe whispered to her, continuing to smile and wave at the audience. "He's so cute."

"That's him."

"How's he doing? He's not sick anymore?"

"He's fine as long as he doesn't race, Chloe. As you can see, he's still got a broken ankle."

"Can you believe it? Some kids are crazy enough to keep racing after an accident like that. Mike Mitchell . . ."

Mechanically, Alison kept throwing flowers while Chloe told her about Mike Mitchell, who apparently had been in critical condition for weeks and went back to motocross as soon as he could walk again.

"Just like Evel Knievel, who's broken every bone in his body," finished Chloe.

Finally the parade was over. Floats clustered in the supermarket parking lot, and friends and parents crowded around them. Alison jumped off her float.

"Hey, you almost jumped on my feet."

Billy appeared in front of her. He waved his paper flower in front of her and smiled uncertainly. "You want my other foot in a cast?"

Alison groped for words, and Billy spoke before she could say a word. "Can we talk?"

Families moved in around the queen and princesses. Everyone was occupied. Alison figured this was as good a time as any.

"OK."

They strolled away from the float, and Billy started talking.

"I know why you're upset with me. I guess you must think I'm going to start racing again, after I told you I wouldn't."

"That's right."

"Well, I'm not racing again. I can't. I'm not stupid, Alison. But I can ride a bike to test it out, which was what I was doing yesterday. I designed a new type of shock absorber for rear tires, which I want to sell to Johnnie's Cycle Shop."

"But you're not supposed to ride at all, are you? What about your kidney?" She hoped she didn't sound too dramatic.

He shook his head. "Do you want to talk to my doctor? I can ride, just not compete. I can't ride over jumps. You know, the rough stuff. But I can hang around the track all I want."

"Those guys at the track—"

"They're all good racers, and they're anxious to see me go back in full force. They don't know what I've been through."

Alison surveyed his sincere expression. Clearly he was being honest with her. She was wrong—wrong for doubting him, wrong for thinking he would lie to her, wrong for thinking that he wasn't strong enough to resist the thrill of racing.

"I thought that because you loved racing so much, you would go back to it eventually. Most racers are pretty addicted to the track." Alison tried to explain herself. "I've been around racing long enough to know that if you can't take the danger, you have to get out of it. I would never want to change you, Billy, you must know that. Then you'd be somebody else, and I love who you are."

"I know you'd never try to change me. That's one of the things I love about you." He fingered the ribbons in her hair. "And I also know that if it wasn't for Marty, you wouldn't feel this way about racing. Believe me, I don't want to change anything about you, either."

He leaned forward and brushed his lips across hers. "Your hair looks almost as good in ribbons as it does with car grease in it. Did I tell you, you looked beautiful on the float—better than the queen and princesses?"

"No—but don't tell them that." Alison giggled, thinking how horrified Heather would be by that comment.

Billy threaded the paper flower into her long hair and kissed her again. Alison's doubts and fears vanished as his arms closed around her.

Chapter Thirteen

"Can you hand me that wrench, Alison?" Billy called from under the hood of his truck.

"Sure, boss." Smiling, Alison handed him the tool. He was adjusting the carburetor on the truck. She had her eye on his slender form leaning over the fender, and she wanted to reach out and hug him.

She was deliriously happy. Billy was happy working on motorcycles. The people at Johnnie's Cycle Shop liked his ideas and were going to buy some of his designs. After that good news, he had told Alison, "I feel as thrilled now as I used to when I would do a good jump at a race."

Alison also noticed a change in herself. She was forgetting about Marty. Not forgetting, exactly, but his memory was taking a backseat to Billy now.

She had spent an afternoon one weekend cleaning out her closet. She took all the memorabilia from her days with Marty and piled it in the center of the room—trophies, photos, play programs, a pressed carnation he'd given her for the spring prom. She kept two pictures on her bureau, just to refer to once in a while, but the rest she put into an empty boot box, which she placed in a corner at the top of her closet.

"I think that's it." Billy straightened up and wiped his hands on his jeans. There was a streak of oil on his nose. "Let's test-run this thing."

As Alison hopped into the truck beside him, she was slightly nervous about whether or not the engine would run smoothly. Lately, there had been some problems with the engine that she and Billy had put in together, and they had been spending their free time getting it to work perfectly. Now they would see if their work had been successful.

That first date, putting the engine in with Billy, seemed ages ago as Alison took in his familiar profile—the cap pulled down over his brow, the firm mouth that generally wore a hint of a smile. And she recognized his expression of concentration as he listened to every sound of his engine.

They drove in silence until they were both satisfied that the truck sounded right.

"The truck's fine," said Billy. Alison let out a whooping cheer.

"In fact," continued Billy, "I can tell this truck is very happy by the direction it's headed."

"And what direction is that?"

"To Mickey's Ice-Cream Parlor. See? It's got a mind of its own. It's turning into the shopping center, and now it has even found its own parking place." Billy slid out and offered Alison his hand. "Here, m'lady."

"Why, thank you, sir."

They ordered ice cream and sat outside on the curb, happily licking their cones. Billy's cast stretched out on the blacktop, and Alison read her signature on it: "To Billy, the bravest guy I know. Love, A."

She glanced up to find Billy looking at her. He wrapped a strand of her hair around his little finger.

"Let me taste your butter pecan," he said.

Alison held out her cone, but his mouth moved past it. Suddenly he was kissing her.

"Hmm, tastes good." He laughed at her surprise. "Want to try the chocolate chip?" Expecting another kiss, she raised her lips.

This time Billy handed her his cone. Always the unexpected with him, she thought fondly. As she went to taste it, she noticed a flattened surface on the double scoop. Inscribed in melting letters were the words, "I LUV U."

Alison laughed and with her pinky finger scrawled on her own cone, "ME 2."

Sweet Dreams ®

We hope you enjoyed read-
ing this book. All the titles
currently available in the Sweet
Dreams series are listed on the
next two pages. Ask for them in
your local bookshop or news-
agent. Two new titles are published each month.

If you would like to know
more about Sweet Dreams, or if
you have difficulty obtaining any
of the books locally, or if you
would like to tell us what you
think of the series, write to:—

United Kingdom
Kim Prior,
Corgi Books,
Century House,
61-63 Uxbridge Road,
London W5 5SA,
England

Australia
Sally Porter,
Corgi and
Bantam Books,
26 Harley Crescent,
Condell Park 220,
N.S.W., Australia

Love can be rough . . .

ON HER OWN

Suzanne Rand

Most of the kids in the Roughing It Program seems to have a lot more experience and confidence than Katie Carlisle. She wonders if she'll be able to keep up as they learn survival skills for three weeks in the Adirondack wilderness. But Lisa, who becomes Katie's instant best friend, is more than willing to lend a helping hand whenever Katie hits a snag.

Then Jake Summers begins to take an interest in Katie, and Lisa's attitude quickly changes. It's obvious that she and Jake had something going in the past and that Lisa is still in love with him.

Katie is crazy about Jake, but she doesn't want to hurt Lisa. Still, there's something about Lisa's confession of her romance with Jake that doesn't quite ring true.

She had to compete against the boy she loved . . .

RHYTHM OF LOVE

Stephanie Foster

When Scott tells Darcy he doesn't need her as keyboard player anymore, Darcy can't believe it. The band is the most important thing in her life – next to Scott. Now she'll never get to be his girlfriend.

Or will she? What if Darcy starts her own band? Scott will *have* to notice her. As fast as she can, Darcy sets up auditions and forms her own group. But Scott's not the only one who notices her. Carl, her new group's drummer, does too. And Carl is the one who's there to help her when Scott tries to keep Darcy's band from becoming as popular as his own.

THE SWEET DREAMS BEAUTIFUL HAIR BOOK
Courtney DeWitt

Are you happy with your hair?

If your hair sometimes seems like your own worst enemy, don't despair. THE SWEET DREAMS BEAUTIFUL HAIR BOOK has all the secrets to help you stop fighting your hair and start flaunting it:

Step-by-step instructions for getting your hair into shape and finding the cut that's right for you.

Tips for using the tools of the trade – from brushes to blowdriers to curling wands.

The latest techniques for braiding, knotting, rolling, and wrapping your hair.

Fabulous hair accessories you can make quickly and easily – and inexpensively.

Whether your hair is thick or thin, curly or straight, fine or coarse, blond or brunette – or somewhere in between – THE SWEET DREAMS BEAUTIFUL HAIR BOOK will solve your hair-care problems and help you make the most of your natural beauty.

HOW TO TALK TO BOYS
And Other Important People

Catherine Winters

Talk is Sweet . . .

> *When you meet a boy you like, are you too tongue-tied to talk?*
>
> *If he asks you out, do you blush and giggle – and forget to say yes?*
>
> *Do your hang ups keep you from calling that special boy?*
>
> *Can you tell if a boy likes you?*
> *Say no and mean it?*
> *Break up and still be friends?*

Sweet Dreams HOW TO TALK TO BOYS has the answers to all your questions on how to start the conversation flowing, keep his interest growing, and get the romance going. It will even help to keep peace with your family, talk to your teachers, and get along with your friends. With this book and a little practice, in no time at all you'll be one sweet talker.